Jackson went to open the driver's side door for her, but she didn't get in. Instead, she surprised him by placing a hand on his shoulder.

"I'm glad you were at the dinner tonight. I wasn't sure you would be."

"I didn't want to be," he admitted. "Corb pretty much twisted my arm."

"Was it because of Olive that you didn't want to come? Or me?"

"A little of both."

"Ouch. Brutally honest, aren't you?"

"I didn't say that to hurt your feelings."

"Oh. So it was a compliment then?"

"Damn it, Winnie. It's complicated." She couldn't know how hard this was for him. If only he could see her the way he saw Laurel, or Cassidy, or even B.J.'s new wife, Savannah. They were all beautiful women, too.

But only Winnie set his blood on fire. And it was so, so wrong. It had been wrong when Brock was alive. And it was just as wrong now that he was gone.

Dear Reader,

Welcome back to Coffee Creek, Montana, where the Lamberts—a family of ranchers and cowboys—own the largest spread in Bitterroot County, all controlled by matriarch Olive Lambert. Winnie Hays and her new baby have just returned to town and they're about to attend the double wedding of Cassidy Lambert and Dan Farley *(Her Cowboy Dilemma)* and B. J. Lambert and Savannah Moody *(Promise Me, Cowboy)*.

Eighteen months ago Winnie's fiancé was killed in a car crash while he was on his way to their wedding. Winnie has spent a year and a half grieving, but now it's time for her to resume her life in Coffee Creek—and to introduce her son to his father's side of the family.

Dreading Winnie's return is the Lamberts' foster brother, Jackson Stone. He's never told anyone about his secret passion for his deceased brother's woman—a passion that makes him feel all the more guilty for having been the driver during the accident that killed him.

This is the last of my four-book Coffee Creek, Montana series. As a writer it's always difficult to leave behind a community of families and friends who've begun to feel so real you want to send them cards at Christmas! But with the latest developments between Olive and her estranged sister Maddie, it just feels like the right time to close the door on the Lambert family...and await the next writing adventure.

If you'd like to see the pictures that inspired my Coffee Creek, Montana books, visit my boards on Pinterest—my account is named CJ_Carmichael. To find out what I'm working on next, check my blog on my website: www.cjcarmichael.com. I've posted a map of Coffee Creek there, too.

Happy reading,

C.J. Carmichael

BIG SKY
CHRISTMAS

—

C.J. CARMICHAEL

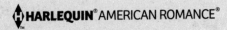
HARLEQUIN® AMERICAN ROMANCE®

Recycling programs
for this product may
not exist in your area.

ISBN-13: 978-0-373-75474-8

BIG SKY CHRISTMAS

Copyright © 2013 by Carla Daum

Printed in U.S.A.

www.Harlequin.com

ABOUT THE AUTHOR

Hard to imagine a more glamorous life than being an accountant, isn't it? Still, C.J. Carmichael gave up the thrills of income tax forms and double-entry bookkeeping when she sold her first book in 1998. She has now written more than twenty-eight novels for Harlequin and invites you to learn more about her books, see photos of her hiking exploits and enter her surprise contests at www.cjcarmichael.com.

Books by C.J. Carmichael

HARLEQUIN AMERICAN ROMANCE

HARLEQUIN SUPERROMANCE

*Harts of the Rodeo
**Coffee Creek, Montana
#Return to Summer Island
***Three Good Men
##The Fox & Fisher Detective Agency

With love to Mike for sharing in
all my Montana adventures

Chapter One

Winnie Hays looked up at the white church and hesitated. She couldn't believe she was here, back in Coffee Creek, Montana. This was her last chance to back out. Everyone would understand if she did.

Since when is wimping out your style? Is that the kind of woman Bobby needs as his mother?

Since the death of her fiancé, that was how she had found the strength to go on. By thinking of their son. And putting his needs before hers.

Still, it was impossible not to recall the last time she'd been here. Wearing a long white gown. Expecting to leave a married woman.

Eighteen months had passed since then, a relatively short period of time marked by the most major events of Winnie's life: the death of her fiancé and the birth of their son seven months later.

She checked her cell phone, making sure it was set to vibrate so she'd know if Bobby's babysitter called. Not that she was worried. Eugenia Fox had raised a son of her own, and had worked for Winnie at the Cinnamon Stick Café since it had opened several years ago.

No, Eugenia and Bobby were going to be fine.

It was herself she was worried about.

If she hadn't been so late, she wouldn't be forced to enter the church alone. Her best friend, Laurel, and her new husband, Corb Lambert—the brother of Winnie's late fiancé—had planned to be by her side for moral support. But they must have given up on her. Decided she'd chickened out.

And she still could. There was no one around to see if she just about-faced and scurried home to the sweet toddler who was the center of her universe.

She sighed.

It was precisely because of Bobby that she needed to attend this wedding. This was his father's family. *Her son's* family. And it was time she faced them.

Still, she paused one last time before entering the church, glancing over her shoulder at the small town of Coffee Creek.

The November day was sunny, crisp and cold. A dusting of snow had decorated the day nicely for the wedding party, the silvery-white crystals contrasting vividly with the blue Montana sky. Olive Lambert, control freak that she was, would be pleased.

Be nice, Winnie. No catty comments about Bobby's grandmother, please.

She grasped the handle, took a deep breath then pulled open the door.

The sound of the organ music almost did her in.

At least it was a different song than the one that had played a year and a half ago. Beethoven was a genius, but she never wanted to hear "Ode to Joy" again.

She peeled off her gloves and tucked them into the pocket of her red wool coat. An usher appeared then, a young man in a cheap suit that didn't fit him well. Winnie remembered him as a cousin on the Lambert side.

"Hi, Adam. Sorry I'm late."

His eyes went wide as he realized who she was. "No problem." He hung her coat for her, then offered his arm. "Come on, I'll show you to your seat."

Winnie schooled herself to look only straight ahead as she walked the length of the aisle. Oh, why had she arrived so late? Now everyone was watching her and there were so many people. Of course there were. The Lamberts owned the largest ranch in the county. They *mattered.* And her son was one of them. So she couldn't break down and cry, she just couldn't. Not even one little tear.

Adam stopped and gestured for her to take a seat in a pew that already seemed to be full. But room was made and she slid onto the wooden bench, not taking note of the person beside her until after she was in position, purse tucked at her feet, tissue palmed discreetly… just in case.

Only then did she notice the masculine thigh pressed next to hers. Looking up, she met Jackson Stone's dark blue eyes. Jackson had lived with the Lamberts since he was thirteen, so he'd been like a brother to Brock, Corb, B.J. and Cassidy. If she'd married Brock, he would have been a de facto brother-in-law to her.

But that didn't mean she knew him well.

Compared to his foster siblings, Jackson was quiet and reserved. Brock had speculated that hardships from Jackson's childhood and early teens had left scars that time might never heal.

And that may well be the case. But at least the man was handsome, with thick dark hair and bone structure good enough to be a model. Weathered skin and the rough look of his hands made it plain, though, that he was a working man.

According to Laurel, Jackson blamed himself for the accident, since he'd been driving, with Brock in the front seat next to him and Corb in the rear. One of the missions Winnie had set for herself on returning to Coffee Creek was to help Jackson see that there was no rational reason for him to feel guilty, and that she, certainly, bore him no malice.

But this wasn't the place for that conversation.

"Hi, Jackson." She smiled and gave him a one-armed hug, which he awkwardly returned.

"Winnie."

He'd never been a big talker. "Big day, isn't it? Double wedding and all."

"Yup."

"Can hardly contain your excitement, huh?"

Jackson's lips curved up a little. "Weddings aren't my thing."

Not hers, either. At least, not anymore. She scanned the line of attractive men standing at the front of the church. There was the local vet, Dan Farley, a solid, muscular guy with sharp cheekbones and dark, almost black eyes. Farley was marrying Cassidy Lambert today.

Cassidy's brother B.J. stood next to Farley. Taller, thinner, he was the only Lambert who didn't share the blond hair and green eyes that Brock had had.

B.J. was marrying Bitterroot County's sheriff, Savannah Moody. Dark haired, sultry-eyed Savannah had been the one who had come to the church to let them know about the accident.

She'd been on duty then. Though she'd been B.J.'s

high school sweetheart, she hadn't been invited to the wedding, due to a longstanding rift between them.

But with the solving of an old case involving arson, theft and murder, they'd resolved their differences. And now they were getting married.

It was an amazing story, and one Winnie had heard secondhand from her friend Laurel as Winnie had still been living in Highwood with her parents at that time.

Moving back to Coffee Creek had been a recent development. So much was the same. And yet so much had changed…

Winnie squeezed the tissue, suddenly wishing she'd brought more. She didn't know how she was going to handle watching Savannah walk down the aisle today. But she had to.

"This must be difficult," Jackson whispered.

Had he noticed her nerves? She nodded.

"Imagine you're at the rodeo." She could feel his breath on her hair as he leaned in to whisper, "Everyone's in regular clothes. The guys are in the chutes, waiting for their ride."

"And the organ music?"

"That's just the fans cheering."

He was being silly. But it was working. She could feel her muscles relaxing. She closed her eyes, picturing the scene that Jackson was laying out for her. She'd been to countless rodeos over the years; in fact, that was how she'd met—

Brock.

Her eyes flashed open. Her heart began to race and her body went rigid. If he hadn't died in that crash on his way to the church, he would be sitting beside her right now. They'd be man and wife and—

The music changed then, became a march. Everyone shifted in their seats, and after a second, so did Winnie.

"Rodeo princesses are making their entrance," Jackson said softly as the crowd gasped. He placed a steady hand on her shoulder.

Her nerves calmed at his words, his touch.

"Imagine they're on horses," he added.

Not hard to do, since the first bride was Cassidy, and she was never happier than when she was riding. The golden-haired woman with her sunshine smile had a degree from the University of Montana but she worked at Monahan's Equestrian Center now, doing what she'd been born and raised to do—train horses.

The normally taciturn Farley beamed as his bride—no, rodeo princess—gave him her hand. The look they shared was so sweet that Winnie's heart tumbled a little, but she set it right again by turning to look at the second bride.

Fortunately, Savannah didn't look anything like a sheriff today in her fitted white dress and delicate shoes, her long dark hair falling in gentle waves down her shoulders. The crowd gave her a second appreciative gasp, but she didn't seem to notice. Her smile and gaze were just for B.J.

As the congregation settled down, Winnie focused on her hands clasped in her lap.

"Family and friends," intoned the minister, "We are gathered today to celebrate the marriages of two very special couples—"

A tear dropped onto her hand. She hadn't even realized that she'd started to cry. She blinked, and a second one followed.

Suddenly a large hand covered both of hers. She felt the rough calluses first. The warmth second.

She glanced up and saw such a tender look in Jackson's eyes that she almost started crying again. Thank goodness she'd been smart enough to forgo eye makeup. She had to get a grip here. Listening to the minister had been a mistake. She had to take Jackson's lead and pretend she was somewhere else.

In her mind Winnie started going over all of Bobby's milestones. The first time he rolled over. His first smile. His first tooth. Gradually she could feel her muscles relaxing, and Jackson must have felt the same, because he gave her hands a pat, then returned his hand to his own thigh.

The fact that he was being so kind to her made her feel even worse about the suffering she knew he'd been going through this past year and a half. She should have called him sooner. Maybe they could have helped one another through their grief, rather than dealing with the sadness and loss on their own.

Once the ceremony was over, they would talk. She'd invite him for coffee. Make things right.

JACKSON STONE WAS in agony. Of all the people in this church, why had that damn kid sat Winnie Hays next to him?

If only they weren't squished in so tightly that he could feel her warm thigh up against his. The contact was the sweetest form of torture he could imagine. There were at least a dozen reasons why he shouldn't find her so attractive, but he did.

And he had from the first time Brock had brought her home to meet the family.

He'd never met a woman before with such sparkle in her eyes, such sass in her smile. He'd watched her shake hands with Olive, Cassidy, Corb and B.J. and when it came time for his turn, he'd half expected sparks to ignite when her palm met his.

And they had.

But only for him.

That was when he knew that he had to keep as much distance between himself and Brock's girlfriend as possible.

And he'd done it.

But it hadn't made his life easy. And it had become a true nightmare on the day of their wedding.

Jackson still had terrible dreams about the crash. He hadn't seen the moose in time to avoid a collision. There had been a curve in the road, then the stand of aspen and willows.

And suddenly the huge body of a bull moose coming up from the right...

No. He couldn't let himself go there. Not now. If this was hard for him, it had to be four times more difficult for Winnie. Last night at the rehearsal dinner Laurel had confided to him that she expected her friend to bail out of the ceremony.

"She'll come to the reception," Corb's redheaded wife had said. "But not to the church."

"Yeah. That's probably the best thing," he'd said.

He'd wished he could skip the ceremony, too. But he'd lived with the Lamberts since he was thirteen, and B.J. and Cassidy were like his own siblings. He didn't want to miss their special day because of his own weakness. And he did see it as a weakness—that he couldn't seem to get past that day.

Diversions helped. Things like work, Maddie Turner's illness and the financial challenge of turning around the fortunes of the Silver Creek Ranch.

But occasionally a guy had to stop and just be.

And that was when the bad memories would sneak in. Sometimes he envied Corb, who'd sustained serious brain trauma in the accident and remembered nothing.

He wished he could have been unconscious, too. Then he wouldn't have the pictures of the awful aftermath in his head.

The split second when he'd seen the moose. Then the crash and the screams. Followed by silence.

The moose had taken out the roof of the truck and sunshine had beamed directly on his head. He'd been pinned to his seat by the airbag at first. Stunned.

The first thing he noticed was the sunshine, warm on his head. Birds were singing. He said a prayer before turning his head.

But the prayer hadn't been answered. Because all he'd seen was blood. And when he'd called out to the others, to Brock and to Corb—no one had responded.

Chapter Two

Olive Lambert was making a toast, welcoming her new son- and daughter-in-law into the Lambert family. All the wedding guests were gathered in the dining hall of Monahan's Equestrian Center. The room was spacious and well-appointed, with windows looking out at rolling hills and distant mountains, a huge river-rock fireplace and a large dance floor next to the bar.

Winnie was enjoying her glass of champagne, which she'd already raised three times for earlier speeches. First Dan had toasted his bride, then B.J. had done the same for Savannah.

Corb, as best man, had spoken next.

And now, Olive.

Winnie tried to remember the last time she'd had champagne. It must have been at her and Brock's engagement party. Unknown to her at the time, that had been when Corb had fallen in love with her best friend, Laurel Sheridan, who'd flown in from New York so she could be Winnie's maid of honor.

The visit had been planned to last one week.

But after Brock's accident, Laurel had extended her stay so she could look after the Cinnamon Stick while Winnie recuperated on her parents' farm in Highwood.

"...I remember when you were just a boy, hanging out with B.J., Corb and Brock," Olive was saying, her gaze on Dan Farley, who had taken over his father's vet practice several years earlier. "You were over so often, it was like you were a member of the family. Now it's official, and I couldn't be more delighted."

"To Dan." Winnie raised the delicate crystal flute and took another sip.

"And of course I want to welcome Savannah to the family, as well," Olive concluded.

Thud. Winnie glanced around to see if anyone else had noticed Olive's lack of enthusiasm toward her new daughter-in-law. Laurel caught her eye, then winked.

Winnie struggled not to laugh. She finished her champagne, set down the glass then moved closer to her friend.

"I guess Olive was hoping B.J. would do better?" asked Winnie. Which, in Olive's mind, meant marrying a local ranching girl whose father owned lots of land.

Laurel was in a forest-green sheath that showcased both her slender figure and her gleaming red hair. "Yes. Savannah is an amazing woman and a terrific sheriff. But her parents had some troubles—financial and otherwise—and Olive doesn't approve."

"Bad bloodlines, huh?"

"Yup. Olive thinks she should be able to control the breeding lines of her children, the same way she does the quarter horses."

Winnie chuckled. Laurel was great at seeing the humorous side of almost any situation. When she was in the early stages of her romance with Corb, Olive had actually invited one of Corb's old girlfriends to dinner, hoping to divert his attention. Winnie would have ex-

ploded in a similar situation, but Laurel had somehow
dealt with it.

"It's crazy, but I guess Olive gets her way sometimes.
Witness Cassidy and Dan Farley."

"That almost backfired on her," Laurel whispered
back. "Didn't I tell you about the ranch getting quar-
antined?"

"Probably. I've been so sleep deprived lately, my
memory is shot." She searched the crowds until she
found Jackson. He was talking with a couple of local
ranchers, but as soon as she spotted him, his gaze met
hers.

She felt the oddest warmth steal over her. Quickly
she glanced away. "What's up with Jackson? Why didn't
he bring a date?"

"Who would he bring? He's been all work, no play
since—"

Laurel didn't finish. She didn't need to.

"Do you think it would help if I talked to him?"

"You can try. Most everyone else has. Except Olive,
of course. She's the only one in all of Coffee Creek who
really does seem to blame him for what happened." Laurel rolled her eyes at the unfairness of it all.

Before Winnie had a chance to reply, the band started
playing and Corb claimed his wife for a dance.

Winnie watched the pair walk off, hand in hand.
They were so good together. Would she and Brock have
been as well suited? She'd never know.

Winnie turned and headed to the bar to get a glass
of cranberry and soda. There were still a few people
she ought to talk to, then she'd go home. She'd told Eugenia that she wouldn't be out very late.

Once she had her drink, she swiveled back toward

the dance floor—and found herself face-to-face with Olive.

The matriarch of the Lambert family was looking her best tonight. Her silver hair was beautifully styled and her trim figure looked sharp in a vintage Chanel suit. Olive always managed to look like a lady—even when she didn't act that way.

"I haven't had a chance to welcome you back to Coffee Creek." The words were nice, but Olive's eyes were cold.

Winnie accepted the tepid hug Olive offered, catching a hint of classic Chanel No. 5 perfume as she did so. "Thanks, Olive. I was wondering if you'd like to pop in at the café next week to meet Bobby."

"My grandson, you mean." Olive's green eyes glittered with affront. "I must say I was surprised—and hurt—that you never sent us a birth announcement."

Trust Olive to make an issue of this, here, in public. "I did call," Winnie said.

"Your message said nothing about having a baby! We had no idea you were even pregnant."

Winnie pulled every inch she could out of her spine. This woman had intimidated her at one time, but no longer. "Well, you would have if you'd returned my earlier call, after Brock's funeral."

Olive's eyes dulled. "That was a terrible time. I wasn't up to talking on the phone."

"It wasn't a great time for me, either." And yet she'd made the effort to get in touch with her fiancé's mother, even though she knew Olive didn't like her. She'd hoped they could come together in their shared grief over Brock's death. And she'd wanted to break the news about her pregnancy in a more personal way, not through a generic birth announcement.

But Olive hadn't called back. And a month later Winnie had tried again, with a similar result.

"You could have written. Or sent word via Corb or Laurel."

"I could have," Winnie agreed. "But you may have guessed by now that I have a stubborn streak."

She met Olive's glare without backing down. The honest truth was she still resented Olive for being so cold toward her. She knew—because Brock had told her—that Olive had tried to talk him out of marrying her. Olive had thought that her youngest, and favorite, son was making a mistake in marrying a simple farm girl from Highwood. Brock had laughed about it later, when they were alone.

But she hadn't.

"I was trying to save you and Brock *both* a lot of heartache. You weren't suited for each other."

Winnie's heart raced. This woman was unbelievable. Like a snake, she struck quickly with her venom. "You can't know that. He loved me. And I loved him, too."

A drop of soda spilled onto her foot. Realizing her hands were shaking, she put her glass on a nearby table. She wanted to leave. But Olive had her cornered.

And she wasn't finished.

"You don't have any idea what it takes to be a rancher's wife. You couldn't have—"

Suddenly Winnie spotted a familiar figure, a man in a dark gray suit. He was headed for the bar, but he didn't seem to have noticed her. She put out her arm and managed to snag a bit of his sleeve.

Jackson turned.

"You wanted to dance? We'd better do it now, since I have to go home early."

Jackson's gaze went from her to Olive. The widowed mother of four children—three, now that Brock was gone—had two spots of red burning on her cheeks.

"We aren't finished here, Winnie," Olive said.

"If you want to meet my son, then I think we are."

Winnie kept her hold on Jackson and pulled him toward the dance floor. Sensing his reluctance, she figured he didn't like to dance.

"Sorry to drag you out here," she said, once he'd swung her into his arms with surprising finesse. "Olive was in attack mode and I needed to escape."

"No one does attack mode quite like Olive."

Jackson was two-stepping like a pro—why didn't he like dancing when he was so good at it?

She glanced up at his handsome face. His gaze was fixed across the dance floor, almost as if he didn't want to look at her. "You two don't get along, either, do you?"

According to Brock, when his father decided to take Jackson in under the foster-care program, Olive had been opposed to the idea.

Dad almost never went against her wishes, Brock had said. *But that time he did.*

"No, we don't. It's one of the reasons I decided to go work on Silver Creek Ranch," Jackson allowed, swinging her out, then pulling her back in.

"Holy cow, you're good at this." He led with assurance and moved perfectly with the beat.

"So are you."

"It's easy when you have a good partner."

Jackson's eyes narrowed. He glanced away again.

"So tell me about Silver Creek Ranch." She needed to

distract herself from how nice his hands felt on her waist and her shoulder. Silver Creek was owned by Maddie Turner, Olive's sister. The two women had been estranged for decades, since the death of their father.

"It's in tough shape. Maddie is a good person, but a terrible businesswoman. I had to sell some land to raise enough money to begin restocking the herd. Fences need mending, and the barn could use some work, too. But I'm taking it one step at a time."

He didn't mention anything about the promise Maddie had made to him. Winnie knew the details thanks to Laurel. Maddie was suffering from terminal lung cancer and she'd told Jackson that if he came to live with her on the ranch and invested all his savings, she'd leave him everything.

Given that Maddie had no children of her own, it wasn't such an outlandish proposition. But according to Laurel, Olive was furious. She felt the land ought to be going to one of *her* children. Never mind the fact that she hadn't allowed any of them to speak to their aunt when they'd been growing up.

"I'm sure you're very busy. But do you have time to come in to the café for coffee one night next week?"

For the first time Jackson's step faltered. He recovered in the next second, found the beat and pulled her with him back into the rhythm.

"I'm not big on coffee."

Was that why in the past he'd come so seldom into the Cinnamon Stick?

"Or cinnamon buns, either, I assume." The buns were the specialty of her café, baked fresh every morning by a former cowboy and recovering alcoholic who'd turned over a new leaf in his sixties, Vince Butterfield.

"Not much of a sweet tooth," Jackson agreed.

"Well." Was he just making excuses? "Maybe you could drop by just to talk, then?"

He swung her out, gave her a twirl and then swirled her back a little, just as the song ended. A few people dancing near them clapped.

"Nicely done, Jackson." Corb had Laurel in his arms and they were both grinning.

Yes, nicely done, Winnie had to agree.

Jackson walked her off the dance floor, then dropped his arm. "Thanks for the dance, Winnie. I'm sure I'll be seeing you around."

And that was it? "What about next week?"

He looked off in the distance for a few seconds before meeting her gaze. "I know what you're trying to do here. You want to tell me you don't blame me for what happened to Brock."

"That's right."

"It's nice and charitable of you, Winnie. But can you really look at me and not think, there's the guy who was driving when my fiancé died?"

His blunt words stole her breath. Before she could recover, he was leaning in to say some more.

"Last thing I want is to cause you more pain. Let's just leave it at that, okay?"

And then he was gone, walking toward the exit. She wanted to run after him, but Corb and Laurel were watching, as were several other couples. Better not create a scene.

So she forced a smile and tried to look as though she and Jackson had parted on friendly terms.

But man, was Laurel right. That guy had a serious

chip on his shoulder. And the last thing she was going to do was let him leave it there.

JACKSON WANTED TO LEAVE, but he knew it was too early and his absence would be noted. He stood in the stairwell of the back exit, his body pressed against the wall of cool concrete.

What was wrong with him? Why did he feel this way?

Holding Winnie in his arms, dancing with her, had been the worst form of torture.

He'd tried thinking about cattle prices, the weather, anything except the beautiful, dark-haired woman who was following his moves so perfectly it was almost like having sex.

He groaned.

Sex and Winnie Hays should never be in the same sentence. Brock had been like a brother and a best friend all rolled into one. And here Jackson was lusting after the woman he had loved.

"Hey, cooling down?" Corb had found him. "I'm not surprised. You and Winnie sure worked up a sweat in there."

Another layer of guilt settled in the pit of Jackson's stomach. Soon he'd have no space in there for anything else.

"She looks good, doesn't she?" Corb handed him a beer.

"I guess."

"I think Mom resents it. She'd have Winnie dressed in black, withered to the bone and miserable for the rest of her life."

"Wouldn't be much of a mother to Brock's son if she did that."

"Winnie never could do anything to please Mom." Corb shrugged. "But she's done her share of suffering." Corb looked at him pointedly. He didn't have to say anything more for Jackson to know what he was thinking. Ever since the accident the Lambert kids had been trying to tell him he had no reason to feel responsible for what had happened.

He appreciated their intentions.

But none of them had been in the driver's seat, so they couldn't really understand.

"You liking the work at Silver Creek?"

"It's a challenge," Jackson allowed, glad that Corb had changed the subject. "But we've sold a parcel of land to Sam O'Neil. Come spring I intend to buy a hundred head of cattle and build from there."

"This Sam fellow. Did you meet him? B.J. says he put in an offer for Savannah's land, too."

Jackson shook his head. "Not face-to-face. He'd already signed the papers when I took Maddie to the title office."

Corb finished his drink, then pushed the door open. "We better get back. There'll be a lineup of ladies waiting to dance with you now that they've seen what you can do. Where'd you learn to two-step like that, anyway?"

Jackson smiled. "My mom taught me. Haven't danced in years. Funny how it all came back."

"Your *mom* taught you?"

Jackson didn't speak of her, usually. All the Lamberts knew was she'd gone to jail when he was thirteen. And died a few years later while still incarcerated.

"She wasn't all bad."

"I'm sure she wasn't. She had you, didn't she?"

It was a nice thing to say, but then Corb was a damn fine man that way. A lot like his father had been.

"Keep talking so sweet to me and Laurel will be getting jealous."

Corb laughed, then shoved him in the direction of the dance floor, none too gently. "Laurel knows who gets my motor running. Now get. The ladies await."

Chapter Three

"Who's Mommy's little boy?"

Bobby giggled as Winnie tickled the bottoms of his feet, then pointed his chubby finger at his own chest.

"That's right." She touched her nose to his. "*You* are my little boy." Were all babies this cute? Winnie didn't believe it. Bobby was special. She put on his socks and his adorable sneakers, and as soon as she was done, he started toddling out of her reach.

She sighed. He was such a going concern now that he'd started walking. She chased after him, scooped him into her arms and he giggled again.

She'd lined up a babysitter for weekdays from ten to two, a friend of Eugenia's whose children were grown and out of the house, but not yet married with families of their own.

They were headed to Linda Hunter's now.

She tucked Bobby into his new winter snowsuit, then grabbed the diaper bag she'd prepared earlier that morning. She left her apartment, which was above the café, through the back door and down the fire escape. More snow had fallen on Sunday and again last night, and Bobby wiggled in her arms. He wanted to play with all that cool white stuff.

"Later, honey." Now that he was mobile, she needed to buy him boots, which would mean a trip to Lewistown. If not for the wedding this past weekend, she would have taken him shopping on Saturday.

A black Ford pickup truck turned onto Main Street. She recognized the vehicle even before she spotted Jackson behind the wheel. He had on aviator sunglasses and a dark brown cowboy hat. He slowed as he passed by, but didn't stop.

She'd thought a lot about Jackson since Saturday night. His kind attempt to distract her during the ceremony. How much fun he'd been to dance with. But most of all, she'd thought about his parting words to her. *Can you really look at me and not think, there's the guy who was driving when my fiancé died?*

He hadn't given her time to answer. But if he had, she would have said, *Of course I can.* She'd never thought of him as the man who was responsible for Brock's death. But that was obviously how he thought of himself. How could she change his mind about that when he seemed determined to avoid her?

A lot of locals made a point of stopping by her café when they came to town, but Jackson rarely had and she knew he wouldn't today, either. She didn't buy the excuse he'd given her at the wedding. Maybe he didn't have a sweet tooth. But she had yet to meet a cowboy who didn't love his coffee.

She turned and watched as his truck made a right on Grave Street. He must be headed to either the Lonesome Spur Bar, Ed's Feed Supply or the cemetery. Odds favored the feed supply store. Maybe, just maybe, he'd surprise her and drop in for a coffee when his business was done.

Bobby placed his hands on her face, forcing her to look at him. "Mama go."

She grinned. He'd just strung together his first two-word sentence. "You're a smart boy. Yes, Mama should get going. Linda will be wondering where we are."

She chatted to him about his new babysitter as she walked. She always talked to Bobby as if he could understand everything she said, and who knew, maybe he did.

Linda lived in a ranch-style bungalow on Aspen Street, and she must have been watching for them out the window because she had the front door open as soon as they arrived. Besides her warm, smiling face, they were greeted with the aroma of fresh-baked bread. Linda's brown hair, only slightly streaked with gray, was pulled back with a clip and she was dressed in jeans and a pale pink sweater.

She didn't make the mistake of reaching for Bobby too soon. Instead she said hello and smiled, then pointed to an area where she'd set out some simple building blocks, cars and board books.

Bobby strained to reach them, almost tumbling out of his mother's arms. With a laugh, Winnie set him on the floor.

"I've childproofed this room," Linda told her. "And I have my neighbor's old high chair so I can feed him his lunch. Will he want a nap after that, do you think?"

"He usually does. But I'm hoping to pick him up early since this is his first time at your place." Winnie handed over a sheet with Bobby's schedule that she'd printed last night. Then the diaper bag. "All his food is in here, as well as diapers and a change of clothes if he needs them."

"We'll be fine," Linda said, reassuringly.

Winnie smiled her gratitude, unable to speak because she was suddenly teary. It was hard leaving her baby with a sitter. But she knew Laurel—who'd taken over at the Cinnamon Stick after Brock's death—was ready to hand the reins back to her. Laurel had enough to do taking care of her nine-month-old daughter, Stephanie, helping Corb around the ranch and writing her blog.

Winnie didn't make a big deal out of saying good-bye to Bobby, and Linda eased her transition out the door by distracting him with a super-cool dump truck.

Fifteen minutes later, Winnie was at work in the café's kitchen, chopping vegetables for her chicken-curry soup recipe. At the sound of the door chime she looked up, wondering if she'd see Jackson. But it was Straws Monahan, the owner of the impressive equestrian center where the wedding had taken place last Saturday. The center, about ten miles from town in the opposite direction from the Lamberts' ranch, was one of the county's main employers. Which made Straws, recently widowed and in his sixties, one of the area's most important men.

Dawn Dolan, a young blonde who still lived at home while she took correspondence courses to upgrade her high school marks, asked him in a cheerful voice how he was and what could she get him.

Winnie smiled, pleased with Dawn's friendly approach. She'd hired Dawn, Eugenia and their baker, Vince, years ago when she'd first opened her café, and they'd all proved to be hardworking and loyal employees.

Winnie knew she'd never have been able to keep her

business afloat the past eighteen months if it wasn't for all of them and Laurel.

Dawn and Eugenia had both agreed to work longer shifts during that time. Laurel had left her dream job as an editorial assistant in New York City to relocate in Coffee Creek. And Vince had kept making the cinnamon buns, muffins and fresh breads that kept her customers coming back for more.

Most people were shocked when they discovered that the Cinnamon Stick's delicious baked goods were made by a member of the Cowboy Hall of Fame, but that was one of the things Winnie loved about Coffee Creek. People here just pitched in and did what needed to be done.

She transferred the carrots she'd been dicing into the industrial-size soup pot on the stove. Just as she was reaching for the celery, she heard someone new entering. Hoping again it might be Jackson, she glanced up with a smile.

And had to work to keep it there when she saw Olive Lambert. Bobby's grandmother was dressed in "work" clothes today—pressed jeans, clean boots and a tailored sheepskin jacket. She nodded at Straws. "Good day."

"Sure is. All recovered from the big weekend?"

Olive sighed with satisfaction. "My daughter made a beautiful bride. She and Farley left yesterday for Maui."

"Our sheriff was quite the bride, too," commented Straws, who'd also been at the wedding. "She and B.J. are going to Australia for their honeymoon, aren't they?"

Olive's smile dimmed a little. "They are. Taking an entire month off."

"Well, November is the time to do it."

"I suppose."

"Here's your order, Mr. Monahan." Dawn passed him a to-go cup and a bag with his pastry, then turned to Olive. "What can I get you, Mrs. Lambert?"

"Nothing. I'm here to speak with Winnie."

Hands already washed and dried in anticipation of this, Winnie stepped out from the counter. "Hello, Olive. Why don't we sit down?"

She led Olive to an empty booth at the back. *Relax. Stay calm,* she advised herself. It would be easier, she hoped, to deal with Olive here than it had been at the wedding.

Her café was a warm, welcoming place, painted and decorated in the colors of the foods Winnie loved most: caramel, chocolate, vanilla and, of course, cinnamon. The booths were nestled up to wooden-framed windows that overlooked the picturesque Coffee Creek for which the town had been named.

In the spring and summer, the water had a translucent topaz color, which some more prosaic types likened to the color of weak coffee.

In the winter, though, ice and snow crept up from the banks of the creek, and the cold streaming water looked more gray than brown.

"I was hoping to meet my grandson today," Olive said, without preamble. "Finally."

"I'm sorry if I wasn't clear. Afternoon is the best time for visits. Around two-thirty, after I finish work."

"So where is he now?" Olive glanced around as if expecting to see him.

"At Linda Hunter's. She's his new babysitter."

Olive frowned. "The whole town is going to have met that child before me."

"What are you doing later today?"

"I'll be at home, going over the accounts, probably."

"I could bring him out to Coffee Creek Ranch for a visit."

Olive's eyes narrowed. "Maybe you could stay for dinner?"

Winnie forced a smile. "Sure. When would you like us? We can come anytime after four."

"How about five, then? We'll eat early so you can get Bobby home at a decent time." Olive started to rise, then hesitated. "Maybe you could take a look at Brock's cabin while you're at the ranch. I was thinking it might make a good home for you and Bobby."

Winnie had heard rumors that Olive wanted her and Bobby to live on Coffee Creek Ranch. Years ago Bob Lambert had built three cabins alongside a small lake on the ranch for Brock, B.J. and Corb.

Since Brock's death, his cabin had been vacant—but moving in there had very little appeal to Winnie. "That's a very kind offer. But my apartment is fine for now. Nice and close to work and Bobby's babysitter."

"Corb, Laurel and Stephanie are very comfortable in their cabin. And I'm sure you'd love living so close to them."

That part was true. But it was living near Olive that had her worried.

"Trust me, your son will be a lot happier growing up on a ranch than he would be in town. Don't you think it's what Brock would have wanted?"

Winnie didn't know what to say to that. Olive had a point. Brock probably *would* want her and Bobby to move to his cabin.

"In fact—" Olive's eyes sparkled as an idea struck

her "—why don't I ask Bonny to freshen up the place today and then Corb can drive his truck into town and help you pack? I bet we could get most of your belongings moved tonight."

Tonight.

Tonight?

"But—" Winnie floundered.

"I'll stop in at Molly's Market and pick up some groceries to stock your cupboards and the fridge. And I'm sure—"

"Wait," Winnie finally said. "This is such a kind offer. But may I think about it a few days?"

"What's to think about? I'm not just offering you a place to live, Winnie. I plan to sign over the papers. The cottage will belong to you, free and clear."

It was incredibly generous. And yet, to Winnie, it still felt like a trap.

Olive placed her hand over Winnie's. "You're a mother now. And mothers put their children's needs before their own. I'm sure it's convenient for you to be close to your work. But think about Bobby. Your apartment is just too small. I've had three sons, so I know what boys need, and that's space. Room to play and run and explore."

Winnie stared mutely at Brock's mother. In the back of her mind she registered the fact that the ladies in the booth beside them had left and some new customers had come in. But she didn't look up to see who they were, or if Dawn needed help.

Right now all she could focus on was Olive.

The older woman had hit a nerve when she'd said a mother had to put her child's interests first.

Was she being selfish by not taking Olive up on her offer?

"Maybe when Bobby's older we could move into Brock's cabin," she finally said. "But he's still small. My apartment is fine for now."

Olive must have been so sure she was winning her case. Now her brow furrowed with consternation. "Are you serious? But isn't it a one bedroom?"

Winnie didn't want to answer. Because she knew Olive was right, that she needed a bigger space. There had to be another solution. If only—

And then, suddenly and unbelievably, Jackson was standing by their table. Winnie gazed up from his boots, to his worn jeans, his open jacket, his guarded face. He touched the tip of his hat. "Olive." He nodded to the older woman, then to her. "Winnie."

"Hello, Jackson." Olive's greeting was clipped. She clearly wasn't pleased at the interruption.

But Winnie sure was. "Hi there, Jackson. Why don't you sit down while I bring you both some coffee and cinnamon buns?"

"I didn't come for food," Jackson said quickly. "Just wondered when you wanted me to start work on that second bedroom for the apartment."

She stared at him blankly. But only for a second. And then she smiled. "The sooner, the better."

"This week is looking good. If I got some measurements now, I could have the supplies by Friday."

"Sounds perfect." Winnie turned back to Olive. "Bobby and I are going to be okay for the time being. But I do appreciate your offer. And I will definitely keep it in mind."

Olive gathered her purse, then stood. Her gaze flickered sharply from Jackson to Winnie, then back again. She wasn't a woman who liked losing. And Winnie could tell she wasn't ready to throw in the towel yet.

"We'll talk about this some more over dinner tonight."

It wasn't a question. It was a demand.

"WHAT A HERO. Thank you." Winnie gave Jackson a grateful smile after Olive left the café. "Let me at least get you a coffee for the road."

"It was nothing. Don't bother." She looked so pretty today in a soft blue sweater and jeans. He liked the way she wore her clothes. They hugged her curves without being so tight they looked like they'd shrunk in the wash. Suddenly remembering he shouldn't even be noticing, he raised his gaze and followed her back to the kitchen.

"How did you guess that Olive had me cornered?"

"Been there myself, far too many times."

"That was a brilliant cover story. Wish I could think so fast on my feet." Ignoring his refusal, she poured coffee in a to-go cup, snapped on a cover then tried to hand it to him.

"I don't—"

"—like coffee," she finished. "Right. You're forgetting I know you. I've seen you come in from the barn and head straight to the coffeemaker in the Lamberts' kitchen. Black, right?"

"No thanks," he insisted. Avoiding this place had always taken an enormous amount of willpower on his part. He had a feeling that once he tasted her coffee it would be even harder. "By the way, I wasn't just blowing smoke with that offer."

She put a hand on one of her curvy hips. "What do you mean?"

"I mean I can make you a second bedroom up there."

She looked puzzled. "You can? But have you even seen the apartment?"

She'd invested an inheritance from her grandmother into the building several years ago, after she and Brock were engaged. The charming brick house on Main Street had seemed perfect at the time. She'd opened her café on the main floor and planned to live in the second-floor apartment until the wedding, after which she'd move to the ranch with Brock and find a renter for her apartment.

Things hadn't worked out that way. But that had been the plan.

"Brock showed me around once, before you moved in. There's an L-shaped living room, right?"

She nodded.

"Well, if we built a wall, you could have a separate room for Bobby. It would be small. But then, so is he, right?"

"Are you serious? You'd really do this for us?"

"Sure." He didn't believe he could atone for Brock's death. But he could help his son—not to mention the woman who had been left standing at the altar. In fact, he felt obliged to do so. "It won't take long. A few weeks. And I'd time the work for when you and Bobby are out."

That would be a key part of the arrangement. The last thing he was trying to do here was spend more time with Winnie.

"I'm planning to work every day from ten to two. Bobby will be out at his babysitter's."

"Perfect. I'll come by after morning chores and be back in time for the evening ones." Luckily, being November, there wasn't that much going on at the ranch. And he'd still have evenings to spend with Maddie. The sickly woman was no longer able to go out, and he usually made them supper, after which they played a round of cribbage then watched the news.

It was a simple, unexciting existence. But he felt good, knowing that his presence made a real difference to Maddie Turner's life. Plus the older woman was pleasant company, undemanding even in her poor state of health.

"Let's take a quick look right now. If you have time?"

He hesitated only a second. "Sure."

They went up the back set of stairs to a small landing with a single door. It wasn't locked, and soon they were in Winnie's cheery apartment. Unlike the café, which was decorated in the warm, muted colors of autumn, this space had been painted white. Bright turquoise, tangerine and yellow cushions, and some framed posters on the walls added vivacity and made the space seem very much *hers*.

It didn't take long for Winnie to show him around.

And it took even less time for him to realize that the space really was too small for her and her son. The problem was all the baby paraphernalia. There was a high chair in the kitchen. One of those baby jumping contraptions in the arched hallway. And toys everywhere.

"Sorry." Winnie picked up a fire truck and placed it in a large plastic tub. "We were rushed this morning and didn't have time to tidy up."

"Maybe you should consider Olive's offer. You'd have a lot more room in Brock's cabin."

Winnie glanced around the apartment, then sighed. "It is pretty crazy, isn't it? But can I be honest with you?"

His heart thudded, warning him of potential danger. But he nodded, all the same.

"I loved Brock very much and a part of me probably always will. But I'm twenty-eight years old. I may be a single mother, and that adds complications, but eventually I'm going to want to date again. Who knows, I may even fall in love."

She glanced at her hands, and for the first time Jackson noticed that while she still wore Brock's ring, it was on the other hand now. "I could even get married," she added softly.

Jackson could well imagine all of the above happening. And a dark envy for this unnamed man filled him with a wave of anger. He waited for the emotion to recede. "I'm sure none of the Lamberts expect you to grieve for Brock forever."

"Besides Olive, you mean?"

He grinned.

"I'm sure you're right. They're good people. And Olive is making a generous offer. The cabin is gorgeous and I'd be next door to my best friend…. But can you imagine me inviting a new man out there? How could I possibly start dating right under the eyes of all those Lamberts?"

"I get it." And he did. For as wonderful as the Lamberts were, they could also be overpowering. If she moved out to the ranch, he could well see Winnie's social life being dominated by family events and gatherings.

Much the way his own had been before he moved to Maddie Turner's.

He realized then that he had to make this work for her. He surveyed the room again, then nodded. "We'll put the wall here." He demonstrated with his hands. "And the door here."

Winnie narrowed her eyes. Visualizing. "Yes. I like that idea. Are you sure it won't take too much of your time?"

"Pretty straightforward job, actually."

As long as he kept his distance and didn't start imagining *himself* as the man she might start dating.

Chapter Four

As Winnie drove over the cattle guard on her way to the Lamberts' ranch later that afternoon, the car shook and rattled. She glanced at her son, buckled into his car seat in the back. His eyes were huge, his face serious. "That was fun, wasn't it?"

He returned her smile, obviously reassured that nothing was wrong.

"Those bumps keep the cows from getting off the ranch," she explained. "Now we drive over a bridge and the car will shake again."

The wooden bridge crossed over one of several unnamed creeks on the property. She drove up the final rise, then stopped the SUV and looked down at the snow-covered ranch, remembering the first time Brock had brought her here.

They'd just returned from a camping trip to Yellowstone, where he'd surprised her with a romantic moonlit proposal. He'd been anxious to make an official announcement to his family, but he'd taken the time to stop in this very spot.

"Your daddy was so proud of this place." In her mind she could hear Brock's voice. *This land has belonged to our family since the mid-1800s.*

Winnie had been impressed. Then and now. She'd grown up on a modest farm where they'd had a house, a barn that housed three milking cows, a shop and a shed for the tractor and farm equipment. But Coffee Creek had at least a dozen buildings, all painted white with green metal roofs. The network of outbuildings, pens, chutes and pastures filled the hollow of the wide valley.

The main house had been built higher, perched into a grove of pines with a view of the flat-topped mountain locals called Square Butte. The home was a beautiful log structure, built Montana style with four bedrooms and a large kitchen and family room on the main level. It would have been a comfortable place to raise a big family. But it must feel rather empty to Olive now that she was alone.

To the left, barely visible through a large stand of aspen, was Cold Coffee Lake, where Bob Lambert had built the cabins for his sons.

We're going to raise our children here, darlin', Brock had told her. *Live our lives and grow old together.*

In a movie, music would have foreshadowed the impending tragedy before them. But there had been a romantic country song on the radio at the time and it hadn't crossed Winnie's mind that Brock's prophecy wouldn't come true.

She wiped a tear from her eye. "Well, Bobby. Ready to meet your grandmother?"

He glanced up again at the sound of her voice, then started gnawing his favorite push car. An incoming molar was Bobby's preoccupation today. Fortunately he was too young to share her apprehension for the evening that lay ahead.

It would be a smallish gathering today, since the newlyweds were on their honeymoons. Fortunately Laurel, Corb and baby Stephanie would be there, so they wouldn't have to face Olive alone.

And maybe Jackson? As an honorary member of the Lambert family, he was usually on hand for family occasions.

THE MINUTE WINNIE stepped in the front door, Olive's arms were out for the baby. Thank heavens Bobby didn't make shy. Fascinated with the chunky necklace his grandmother was wearing, he went easily into Olive's clutches.

Um, embrace.

Be nice, Winnie. How often would she have to remind herself to behave tonight?

But it was difficult not to recall her first visit to the ranch, when Olive had flashed her eyes disdainfully over her bargain-basement sundress, mentioned an old girlfriend of Brock's *twice* and barely glanced at the diamond on Winnie's fourth finger when her son gave her their big news.

Winnie rubbed the ring now, hoping this evening would pass much easier than that long ago one had. Laurel kept telling her that Olive wasn't so bad. Maybe she'd grown softer and more understanding in the wake of Brock's death. Not that Winnie had seen any evidence of that so far.

No, more likely easygoing Laurel brought out the best in Olive, while she did the exact opposite.

"Good to see you back here at the ranch." Corb was the first to give her a hug, and Laurel was right behind him. They led her to the family room where Stephanie, two months younger than Bobby and not yet mobile, was playing on a quilt spread over the hardwood floor.

"Gosh, she's so cute." Winnie crouched to give the little girl a kiss. Stephanie glanced up at her, smiled then went back to stacking her colored plastic blocks. "I remember the days when I could put Bobby in one place and he'd stay put."

Laurel nodded. "It's nice. I'm not at all anxious for her to learn how to crawl. Corb's gone crazy baby proofing the cabin. I swear he'd put in rubber walls if I let him."

"Might start a new decorating craze," Corb said.

Winnie and Laurel looked at each other, then laughed.

"It could happen," Corb insisted. "I have other great ideas, too, but before I get to them would anyone like a glass of wine?"

Both Winnie and Laurel said yes, but Olive shook her head. She still had Bobby in her arms. She'd given him a tour of the family room and was now showing him a picture on the fireplace mantel.

"This is your Daddy. Can you say Dad-dy?" Olive broke the word into two syllables and repeated them several times. Bobby stopped gnawing on his toy and stared at her, but he didn't make a sound.

"He doesn't talk much yet," Winnie said. "Just a few words. *Mama* and *go* are his favorites."

Olive didn't acknowledge this, just went back to chanting, "Dad-dy. Dad-dy. Dad-dy. Can you say Dad-dy, honey?"

Corb, Laurel and Winnie exchanged uncomfortable glances.

"Sure smells good in here." Winnie supposed Jackson wasn't coming after all. The dining room table had two high chairs and four place settings.

"Bonny made a chicken stew and biscuits," Laurel said. "It's ready in the oven. We're just waiting for Jackson."

Olive's head snapped up. "I didn't invite him tonight."

"No. But I did." Corb casually added an extra plate and flatware to the table, then pulled up another chair.

The veins in Olive's neck tightened. "I wish you hadn't, son."

"Mom, I know you're upset that he went to work with Maddie. But he's still part of our family."

"He sure isn't acting like it. After all the years we housed and fed that boy, don't you think he owed me more loyalty than going to work for the one person he knows I can't tolerate?"

"You and Dad did a lot for Jackson, it's true. But he worked hard for us when he lived here. I'd say he's settled that score."

"Really? I wonder if Winnie can be so magnanimous, given that Jackson was the one driving when—"

"Mom. Don't. Don't even say it." Corb's voice was so sharp that Stephanie started to cry. Bobby's lower lip trembled, too, and he reached for his mother. When Laurel moved to comfort her child, Winnie was glad of the excuse to reclaim her son from his grandmother's arms.

No one said anything for the next few seconds. And then a knock sounded at the front door.

Talk about perfect timing. Or was it? Winnie eyed Olive apprehensively. Was she going to make a scene? Maybe even tell Jackson he wasn't welcome?

Corb must have been wondering the same thing. The normally good-natured cowboy shook his head at his mother as he moved toward the foyer.

"Be nice, Mom. As far as I'm concerned, Jackson is my brother. That's how Brock felt, too. And he wouldn't want us to shut him out." He glanced at Winnie, who nodded.

"Corb is right," she said. "Brock wouldn't have blamed Jackson." She hesitated. "And I don't, either."

Olive had no opportunity for a rebuttal, because Corb opened the door then and Jackson stepped in, carrying a large poinsettia. He nodded to the group, his gaze resting on Olive. "They were selling these in Lewistown. Fund-raiser for the Eagles. I thought you might like one."

Winnie held her breath, worried how Olive would react to the thoughtful gesture.

The older woman hesitated for a second, then said, "Thank you, Jackson. You can place it on the table by the window."

By the time Jackson had done this, Corb had a beer opened.

"Here, buddy." He clasped Jackson's arm as he passed him the drink.

"Thanks." Jackson said hello to Laurel and Stephanie next. Then he finally turned to Winnie…and the toddler in her arms.

His chest expanded as he drew in a deep breath. "So this is Bobby."

Only then did Winnie realize that while she and Jackson had seen each other several times since her return to Coffee Creek, this was the first time he'd met her son.

Brock's son.

"Hey there, little guy." Jackson's voice was so tender, Winnie felt a lump forming in her throat. "You're pretty darn cute, aren't you?" he added.

"He looks just like his father," Olive said proudly.

Jackson nodded. "But he has his mother's eyes." As he said this, he looked at Winnie, and she felt a moment of connection. *This is as hard for him as it is for me.*

"I'm sure his eyes will lighten up as he gets older," was Olive's comment. Winnie glanced at Laurel, saw her fighting back a smile and she had to do the same. Subtle, Olive was not.

This was Brock's baby, and that was that. Not even his eyes were allowed to be like his mother's.

"Well, now that everyone's here," Corb said, "how about we dive into the chicken stew? Mom, sit down and relax and let us men do the serving."

Olive, not a fan of kitchen duties, didn't have to be asked twice. Once the stew, biscuits and salad had been placed on the table, Jackson and Corb took their seats between Winnie and Laurel. For most of the meal, the talk was of cattle prices and auctions. Olive doted on her two grandchildren, feeding them mashed chicken stew and biscuits, leaving her own dinner practically untouched.

Winnie tried insisting that Olive eat. "Let me worry about Bobby now. Your food is getting cold." She should have known better.

"I can always eat later. My grandson and I have a lot of catching up to do."

After the meal and the pumpkin pie that followed, Olive excused herself from the table. A few minutes later she was back with two huge bags full of baby gifts. Only one small package was for Stephanie. The rest were Bobby's.

"Wow. That's a lot of presents." Winnie was beyond overwhelmed.

"Like I said, I have a lot of catching up to do."

Winnie didn't miss the sharp look of annoyance in Olive's eyes when she said this. But she chose to ignore it.

She and Laurel set Bobby and Stephanie on the floor and the family gathered round for the big unwrapping. The babies were too young, though, and Winnie and Laurel ended up tearing off most of the wrapping paper.

Winnie's own mom and dad had been generous when Bobby was born. They'd bought her his car seat, as well as a crib. But Olive must have spent at least as much money. There were dozens of outfits, as well as a snowsuit, boots, hat and mittens perfect for the Montana winter.

And toys. So many. Most of them related to farming and ranching. Stephanie, too young to feel jealous, or even understand what was going on, reached for one of the plastic horses. Bobby watched placidly, then turned back to the mountain of gifts. His eyes lit up as he spied something special. He crawled over to the miniature Stetson, planted his butt on the floor then stuck the hat on his head.

"Look at that," Corb chuckled. "He even put it on the right way."

When everyone laughed, Bobby beamed then toddled to his mother for a hug and a kiss.

Olive's expression grew pensive. "Look at him. Walking already. I've missed out on the baby stage entirely."

Winnie bit back the sharp comment that almost slipped off her tongue. "My coffee could use a refill." She escaped to the kitchen before she said something she might regret later.

JACKSON WATCHED WINNIE retreat to the kitchen with her spine taut, eyes shining much too brightly. He didn't often find himself siding with Olive, but this one time, he did. Winnie's secrecy about her baby had him puzzled. Why had she waited so long to share her good news with Brock's family?

Thinking he might just refill his own coffee and see how she was doing, he started for the kitchen, but paused when Laurel started defending her friend.

"Olive, I know you feel like you've missed out. But try imagining what the past year and a half have been like for Winnie. The day of Brock's funeral, she had bad abdominal pain and bleeding. She was in and out of doctor's appointments for the next week, and for a while it looked like she was going to lose the baby."

The words hit Jackson with a mighty punch.

Those first few weeks after Brock's death had been hell for all of them. And to think Winnie had been dealing with so much more. And he hadn't had a clue.

"She tried calling you, Olive," Laurel continued. "She might even have driven down and forced you to talk to her. But she couldn't. Her doctor had her on bed rest for most of her pregnancy."

Olive's eyes flickered. She glanced down at her hands, then toward the window. "I'm sorry. I wish I had known. But after the baby was born…"

"Why didn't she tell you then?" Laurel's voice was more gentle now. "It wasn't an easy birth. And then

Bobby had colic. It's taken a long time for Winnie to recover…mentally and physically. Let's not forget that she was also grieving the loss of the man she loved throughout all of this."

Jackson couldn't listen anymore. He left the room, went for the coffeepot then froze. Winnie was still standing there, her mug empty in her hands.

"What's Laurel saying out there?" she asked.

She hadn't turned to look at him, and he studied her profile, the straight line of her nose, the full lips, her small but firm chin. She was such a beautiful woman, and she was strong, too. Much stronger than he had realized.

"She's telling us what you've been through since Brock died." He cleared his throat. "I had no idea you had such a struggle to keep the baby—"

He stopped talking as Winnie turned to him. Her eyes, normally sparkling with good humor, were dark and sad. She glanced from his face to the empty cup in his hand. Automatically she reached for the coffeepot.

He'd been intending to have a refill. Inexplicably he changed his mind and placed the mug in the dishwasher. Laurel joined them, then. It seemed like a good time to make his escape. He wasn't sure what to say, anyway. That he felt badly for her? That he wished he could have helped in some way?

As if anything he could have done would have made a difference.

LAUREL SIGHED AS she reached for the coffeepot. "I had to say something. I couldn't take listening to her badger you anymore." She refilled her mug, then Winnie's.

"Nice of you to try," Winnie said. "But it won't make

any difference. Olive is always going to blame me for this. In a way, she's right. But I just didn't have the strength to handle one more thing."

As she spoke, Winnie watched Jackson head back to the family room, where he took a chair near Corb. She wondered what he'd been about to say to her. Jackson so rarely voiced an opinion that when he did, it was worth taking note.

But he'd left the kitchen now, so she'd probably never know what he'd been thinking.

"Olive is Olive," Laurel concluded the point she'd been making. "At least she's a good grandmother. I'll give her that."

"She sure spoils them with gifts. I'm not sure I'm going to be able to fit all that new stuff in my apartment."

"Maybe you should rethink moving to the cottage. Corb and I would love to have you living next door."

"That part would be fun," Winnie admitted.

"Bobby and Stephanie could grow up playing together."

Winnie groaned. "Stop tempting me."

"Then move in. You know how much I worried about missing New York. But I love it here."

"Sure you do. You're married to Corb. And this is his place."

"Bobby's a Lambert, too."

"Yes, but he's my son, not my husband. I'm not even thirty years old." She hesitated, then added, "One day I might start dating again. Can you imagine how weird it would be for my boyfriend to have to drive out to my deceased fiancé's ranch in order to pick me up?"

Laurel wrinkled her nose. "True enough. Darn. I was

really hoping I could talk you into this. But it's cool you're thinking of dating. Who's the guy?"

"There is no guy. I'm speaking hypothetically."

"There are some awesome single cowboys in the area. I met several when I was working at the café."

Winnie felt not even a spark of curiosity. She'd only brought up the possibility of dating again so her friend would stop pushing her to move out to the ranch.

"Speaking of the café." She grasped the opportunity to change the subject. "I want to thank you again. If you hadn't kept the Cinnamon Stick running while I was laid up at Mom and Dad's, I'd be out of business by now."

"Hey, I would have done it for free. And you insisted on paying me a salary."

"Well, of course. It was the least I could do."

"You've always been there for me when I needed you. And I'm glad I could finally do the same for you."

Laurel was talking about the years when they'd been young girls on neighboring farms in the Highwood area. Laurel had been only eight when her mother died. Left alone with a cool, distant father, she'd been unofficially adopted by the Hays family. The two girls had spent so much time together they were like sisters—except they rarely fought.

"Tell me. Do you think Jackson's doing okay?" Winnie had her eyes on him as she asked this. While he was listening to Corb talk, he was watching Bobby. What was he was thinking? She'd noticed how moved he'd been when he'd met her son earlier. Was it the likeness to Brock that got to him?

Laurel sighed. "Corb's worried about him. We hoped moving to Silver Creek Ranch and working for Maddie Turner might help. But he seems as withdrawn and sad as ever."

"Did you see how choked up he got when he met Bobby?"

"Yes. But so was Corb. And Olive can't take her eyes off him, either."

"I'm a little worried that people are going to expect Bobby to be exactly like his father as he grows up."

Laurel nodded thoughtfully. "I see what you mean. I hate to say it, but maybe you're right to keep a little distance between your son and Coffee Creek Ranch."

And by Coffee Creek Ranch, they both knew she meant Olive.

WHEN THE EVENING was over, Jackson volunteered to load Bobby's gifts into Winnie's car. He wasn't looking for opportunities to be alone with Winnie, but Laurel and Corb had left five minutes earlier when Stephanie started fussing for her nighttime bottle. And he couldn't leave Winnie to manage alone.

The babies had managed to make quite a mess and it took him a couple of trips to get everything in the trunk. By then Olive had said her farewells and Winnie had her son strapped into his seat. By the angle of Bobby's head, Jackson suspected the little guy was already asleep.

Winnie was wearing a red coat that looked great with her dark, wavy hair. The night was clear, the air cold and crisp. Already the tip of Winnie's nose was turning pink.

She waited until he'd emptied the last of the packages, then closed the trunk. "What a lot of loot. And it's still six weeks until Christmas."

"She'll spoil him then, too," Jackson predicted.

"God, I hope not. I don't think I have enough room for all of this, let alone more."

"Maybe I should build in a storage unit in the new bedroom?"

"What an awesome idea."

He went to open the driver's-side door for her, but she didn't get in. Instead she surprised him by placing a hand on his shoulder.

"I'm glad you were at the dinner tonight. I wasn't sure you would be."

"I didn't want to be," he admitted. "Corb pretty much twisted my arm."

"Was it because of Olive that you didn't want to come? Or me?"

"A little of both."

"Ouch. Brutally honest, aren't you?"

"I didn't say that to hurt your feelings."

"Oh. So it was a compliment, then?"

"Damn it, Winnie. It's complicated." She couldn't know how hard this was for him. If only he could see her the way he saw Laurel, Cassidy or even B.J.'s new wife, Savannah. They were all beautiful women, too.

But only Winnie set his blood on fire.

And it was so, so wrong. It had been wrong when Brock was alive. And it was just as wrong now that he was gone.

"I'll come by the café tomorrow afternoon to start work on the new bedroom."

"Are you sure? If seeing me is such a chore, maybe I should hire someone else to do the work."

"Hire? I wasn't asking you to pay me." He sighed. Somehow this conversation had gone completely sideways. "Brock would want me to do this. For the baby. For you. So please let me build you the extra bedroom, Win."

She looked at him as if there was something missing, something she wanted but couldn't find.

He was relieved when she finally turned away.

"Okay, Jackson. I won't say no. You can start the work whenever you want. And I promise to stay out of your way."

Chapter Five

The next morning, Jackson put a pot of coffee on to boil on the big cast-iron wood-burning stove in Maddie's kitchen. It was only eight o'clock, but he'd already finished the chores. They were pretty simple, with only thirty cattle and a half-dozen horses to look after. Hard to believe that at one time the Turner ranch had rivaled that of the Lamberts.

Jackson added another stick of birch to the stove, then halved a couple of Vince Butterfield's cinnamon buns and added slices of cheddar and wedges of apple to each plate.

He took the simple breakfast, including coffee, on a tray to the sitting room, where Maddie was ensconced in the recliner chair that had once belonged to her father. Her border collies, Trix and Honey, were sleeping at her feet. He'd let them out for a romp in the snow earlier, and they were tired now.

Maddie shooed the ginger cat from her lap while he set her plate and mug on the table beside her chair.

"Waiting on me wasn't part of our deal. I'm perfectly capable of getting my own meals." A year ago Maddie had been plump, but she'd lost at least twenty pounds since then, which was a lot considering her short stature. Her once rosy complexion was gray now, as was her short, wiry hair. Only the remarkable green of her eyes had been untouched by disease.

"I know you're capable," he said. But he'd noticed that if he didn't bring her food, she rarely ate. "I was hungry myself, so I figured I might as well bring your breakfast at the same time." He took his plate from the tray, waited for her to take her first bite then made quick work of his.

The cinnamon buns were compliments of Vince Butterfield, who had been cycling out to the ranch every week since Maddie was confined to the house. Vince had lost his driver's license once on a DUI charge and had made a promise to himself then that he'd never get behind the wheel of a car again.

The bike was good enough to get him around town and to and from his trailer, even in the winter. But Coffee Creek Ranch was twenty minutes by car—much too far for a bicycle trip in winter. So Jackson suspected there'd be no more cinnamon-bun deliveries after this last one.

Once upon a time Vince and Maddie had been sweethearts. But Vince had left her to follow the rodeo circuit. He came back to Coffee Creek for visits, but only moved back permanently when a chance meeting with Winnie and the offer of a job at her café had been the motivation he needed to finally stop drinking.

And so he'd moved into a trailer a few miles from town, bought a bike and started a new career as a baker—something he was surprisingly good at.

At first he'd very much kept to himself. But lately it seemed as if he'd like to mend fences with Maddie. Besides the cinnamon-bun offerings, it was Vince who'd

taken care of the cattle when Maddie was first hospi-
talized. That was before Maddie had made Jackson her
preposterous offer.

Jackson's side of the deal was simple. He was to take
over the operations of Silver Creek Ranch, expand the
herd this spring and live in the ranch house, allowing
Maddie to remain in her own home for as long as she
was able. She claimed she didn't need a nurse—and had
no money for one besides—but her doctor had insisted
she was too sick to live alone.

In return for this—which wasn't much in Jackson's
estimation—Maddie was going to leave the ranch to
him when she died. Or so she claimed. He, personally,
still hoped to talk her out of it.

"What's your day look like today?" Maddie plucked
a crumb from her blue housecoat and placed it on the
tray.

"I'm starting work on that new room for Winnie Hays.
I'll pick up some groceries and be home around three."

"Good. I asked my attorney to come out at three-
thirty."

Jackson held out his palm like a traffic cop. "This
isn't about your will, I hope."

"Of course it's about my will. We have to get this
settled. Make our deal official."

"But it's too one sided. I'm not family. You should be
leaving your land to B.J., Corb and Cassidy."

"They'll inherit from their mother."

True. And Coffee Creek was already the largest
ranch in Bitterroot County. But Jackson knew that
Olive had dreams of one day—after her sister's death—
combining the two properties. He'd overheard her talking to her husband about it many years ago.

Bob, who'd been a gentle man with a soft heart, had admonished his wife. "You don't want anything to do with your sister, yet you think she'll leave her land to our children?"

"Who else?" Olive had asked.

Who else, indeed? The last person Olive would have expected, Jackson was sure, was the delinquent boy whom her husband had insisted they take on as a foster child.

"Divide the will between all four of us, then."

"That won't leave you enough for a viable cattle operation. You'd be forced to sell to the Lamberts. And that would be the end of Silver Creek Ranch." Maddie gazed sadly at a picture of her father and mother on their wedding day, which she kept on a bookcase next to the television. "I wish I'd had my sister's head for business. I've practically bankrupted myself. If you can pull Silver Creek out of the red, then you'll deserve your inheritance, Jackson."

He didn't agree. But he didn't want to tire Maddie out with more arguing. He could see her eyes were already getting heavy.

Discreetly he removed her breakfast dishes and carried them back to the kitchen. He couldn't help wondering if there was another reason Maddie was so intent on willing him her family's land. Because, despite her self-admitted lack of business sense, Maddie was no fool. And giving her land to a man she had no connection to just didn't make sense.

Two weeks had gone by. Two weeks of Jackson creeping up the back stairs with his lumber and his tools. And two weeks where Winnie had hardly seen him.

"How much longer until Jackson is finished with his renovations?" Eugenia Fox ran her dusting cloth over the counter of the Cinnamon Stick and showed the soiled result to Winnie.

Eugenia's dark hair was in a bun, as usual. She was widowed, with a grown son who lived in Great Falls but wasn't yet married. Besides working at the Cinnamon Stick, she also ran a part-time catering business.

"He's sanding the drywall today. So this should be the end of it." Winnie knew her staff and customers were ready for relief from the sound of the hammer and the drill and the constant migration of sawdust and plaster particles.

"I've been dusting two times a day since he started." Eugenia tossed the dirty cloth into the laundry bag. "Not that I'm complaining, you understand."

She winked, and Winnie gave her an impulsive hug. "The past two weeks have been a big pain. Thank you for putting up with all the construction."

"What about me?" Vince made a rare appearance from the kitchen. As usual, the wizened old cowboy had a snow-white baker's apron over his jeans and Western shirt. Winnie had never seen him with so much as a single stain on his apron. The man was meticulous.

"Are you fed up with the noise and mess, too?"

"Not really. But I could use a hug, all the same."

For some reason Vince, who kept his distance from most people, even friends he'd known for all his life, had an affinity for Winnie. Maybe because she'd offered him the job that he claimed had saved his life. Since he'd started working at the Cinnamon Stick, he hadn't had a drop of alcohol to drink.

"Any time, Vince. You know that." Winnie gave the

cowboy a grateful hug, then went back to slicing toma-
toes for the luncheon sandwich special. Five minutes
later the rush started, and she and Eugenia were in constant motion pouring coffees and serving sandwiches,
soups and, of course, Vince's famous cinnamon buns.

Around ten minutes to two, Cassidy came in with
her new husband.

"You're back!" Winnie slipped around the counter
to give both Cassidy and Farley a hug. Farley was always dark skinned since he had some Native American blood, but Cassidy had acquired a golden tan on
her honeymoon. "You look great."

"We had a fabulous time in Maui." Cassidy smiled
up at her new husband.

Farley grinned. "It was the best. But we sure missed
our regular coffee breaks. We'll each take a coffee and
a cinnamon bun to go."

As Winnie prepared their order, they filled her in on
all the snorkeling, hiking and sightseeing they'd done
during their holiday.

"It's good to be home, though," Cassidy acknowl-
edged. "Even though it's snowy and cold."

"Must make for quite a change from Maui." Winnie
checked the time. "Oh, wow, how the time flies. I have
to go pick up Bobby from his babysitter's."

By the time she returned, Jackson would be gone.
Ever since he'd started the job, he'd been real careful
to arrive shortly after ten in the morning and leave just
after two, when she was on her way to pick up Bobby.

Just as he'd promised.

Today, though, turned out to be different.

With Bobby in her arms, tired and practically asleep,

Winnie returned from the babysitter's to find Jackson vacuuming drywall dust from the floors.

Her spirits lifted at the pleasant surprise. She was so tired of coming home to an empty apartment all the time.

"Wow. I had no idea men looked so sexy when they vacuumed. I wonder why they don't do it more often."

Jackson's eyes widened, and the word "sexy" hung in the air between them.

Why had she said that?

Maybe because it was true?

Jackson yanked the plug from the wall and the apartment was suddenly silent.

"I wasn't vacuuming. It's called construction cleanup."

"I guess that does sound more *manly*."

"Damn right it does." He grinned. "But I can't say I object to being called sexy." His gaze dropped to Bobby. "Looks like you have a sleepy guy on your hands."

She nodded, her heart suddenly working far too hard. Jackson didn't smile often, but when he did, the effect was disarming. "Can you pull off his boots for me, please?"

"Sure."

Jackson moved closer, tugging off the boots and then setting them carefully on the mat near the door.

Winnie carried her son to his crib where she laid him down, then unzipped his snowsuit and peeled it off his pliable limbs.

Jackson watched, looking fascinated. "Gosh, he's really out, isn't he?"

"Sleeping like a baby," she agreed.

The corner of Jackson's mouth curved upward, but only slightly. "Someone's in a good mood today."

She hadn't been, particularly. Seeing him, though, had changed that. But it wasn't Jackson in particular, she told herself. It was the relief of not coming home to an empty apartment for once. Bobby kept her busy almost every second he was awake, yet there were stretches of time when she felt profoundly lonely up here in their cozy apartment.

It was almost enough to make her regret moving out of her parents' home. Almost.

Truth was, they'd all been getting on one another's nerves the past few months. And it had been time for her to start living an independent life again.

"So how are things going up here? Looks like you're almost finished." Her voice didn't come out sounding natural. She felt suddenly awkward now that Bobby was settled.

The look Jackson gave her was cryptic. Why was the man so darned hard for her to read?

"I am," he agreed, as he moved around the apartment gathering up his equipment. He always left the apartment tidy and clean when he was finished for the day—a consideration that she very much appreciated.

He demonstrated the door that he'd just installed that day, then ran his hand along the new wall. "It's dry and smooth, ready for painting. I can do that tomorrow if you pick out a paint color."

He nodded at the array of paint-color swatches she'd brought home from the hardware store, which were now strewn over the coffee table.

"Oh, don't worry about the painting. I can do that myself."

"With a baby wandering around? Doesn't seem like a good idea to me." Jackson cocked his head to one side and Winnie's heart lurched as she realized she was *attracted* to Jackson.

Seriously attracted.

She thought back to Cassidy and B.J.'s wedding, to the way she'd felt in Jackson's arms as they were dancing. She'd felt it then, too.

Why had she never seen how sexy Jackson was? She'd known it, of course. Had even joked about it when she came into the apartment a minute ago.

But it was one thing to notice how good a man looked.

Quite another to feel the attraction zinging throughout her body, all the way to her fingers and toes.

He was wearing a white T-shirt and jeans today, clothes that showed off every muscle in his cowboy-tough body. He hadn't shaved for a few days, and with his dark stubble and thick tousled hair he reminded her of Joe Manganiello, the actor from *True Blood*.

"Have I got drywall dust on my face or something?"

She'd been staring. Inwardly she cringed as she imagined what Jackson would say if he knew what she'd been thinking. He was already so uncomfortable around her. If she admitted that she really did find him *sexy*?

Oh, man, that would be so bad.

She quickly grabbed the paint samples. "No. Your face is fine."

I'll say...

"I was just thinking about a color to paint Bobby's room. Blue seems so...conventional. What do you think of this turquoise?" She showed him the tiny square and he squinted at it.

"Looks girly."

She sighed. "Well. I guess I'll pick something more neutral. When Bobby goes to bed at eight, I'll get started. In a couple of nights I'll have the painting done."

Jackson looked as if he wanted to argue, but he didn't, thank goodness.

"How's Maddie doing?" She followed him to the door, where he had his supplies stacked and ready to go.

"I'm taking her to the doctor tomorrow. She doesn't complain, but I can tell she's getting weaker." He brushed a hand over his forehead. "Used to be she'd walk her dogs every morning. Lately all she manages to do is move from her bed to the reclining chair in the sitting room."

Thinking of all the hours Jackson had put in on her project, Winnie felt guilty. "I shouldn't have asked for your help. She needs you more."

"You never asked. I offered." Jackson opened the door and stepped out into the icy winter air.

She took a step after him, shivering as the wind cut through her sweater and slapped her cheeks, watching as he started down the stairs with his equipment. "Thank you for building Bobby his bedroom. It's perfect."

Jackson gave her a final nod. And then she shut the door against the freezing wind. Leaning her back against the door for support, she listened to the pounding of her heart and wondered what the hell was the matter with her.

Jackson was practically Brock's brother.

And she had no business at all thinking about him this way.

WOMEN PUZZLED JACKSON sometimes. Like the clothes they wore when they expected to get dirty or stained. Such as the jeans and T-shirt that Winnie had on right now.

He supposed in Winnie's mind they were old and expendable.

But they were pretty much the sexiest things he'd ever seen her wear.

He dipped the roller into the tray, waited for the excess paint to drain away then resumed painting.

He'd dropped by at eight-thirty that evening.

"Happened to be in the neighborhood. Want a hand?"

She'd pretended to be annoyed, but he could tell she wasn't.

"You don't have to do this."

"No. But with two of us, the room will be finished tonight."

She'd tied her dark curls back in a ponytail. Her jeans were so faded, they'd worn away at the knees, belt loops and back pockets.

It was those back pockets that were going to be his downfall. She filled them out so nicely...and damn it, he wasn't supposed to be looking.

She was playing a Taylor Swift CD, volume low so the music wouldn't disturb Bobby. He concentrated on the wall in front of him. She'd chosen a soft gray with blue undertones. He liked it.

"Jackson, what was your life like before you went to live with the Lamberts?"

He supposed she was making conversation, but her question reminded him that they really didn't know much about each other. Probably because he'd always made a point of avoiding her.

"We moved a lot when I was a kid. I was born in Great Falls, but we also lived in Butte and Helena, and for a few months, Bozeman."

"The big city life, huh?"

"The biggest Montana has to offer," he agreed, going along with the joke because the most populated city in this state didn't even come close to half a million people.

Which, in his opinion, was one of the many great things about Montana.

"What did your mom do for a living?"

"She worked nights as a cocktail waitress. We got by okay, until she met a cowboy who got her hooked on crack cocaine again."

"Again?"

"She quit after she had me. Or so she said." He sighed.

He'd skimmed over a lot of territory with that summary. Like the years he'd spent sleeping in the backseat of their car while his mother worked, because she couldn't afford a sitter.

Or the nights she'd bring home some drunk cowboy, and he'd blast the radio in his room so he wouldn't have to hear those embarrassing sounds.

"How did you end up being taken in by the Lamberts?"

"Good question. I never did figure out how that happened. I was thirteen at the time and my mother let herself get dragged into her boyfriend's stupid robbery scheme. The money was going to be for drugs, of course."

Winnie stopped painting for a second, her eyes soft

with sympathy. "Where were you when this was happening?"

"At home. Mom hadn't told me about the plan. I thought they'd gone out to party. Next thing I knew, a social worker and a cop were knocking at the door." He shrugged. There'd been some confusing weeks after that, but then one day a big rancher with broad shoulders and kind blue eyes had shown up at the transitional housing center where he'd been placed.

"Did they take you to see your mother?"

"Eventually. She was so ashamed she wouldn't even look me in the eye. I felt bad for her." But even more he'd been angry. He'd been old enough then that he'd wanted to help look after his mother. He worked two part-time jobs after school and on weekends, making enough to buy his own clothes and contribute to their expenses.

Why hadn't that been enough for her?

Why had she turned to that jerk boyfriend instead?

He'd been really pissed. For a long time.

"So how did you end up with the Lamberts?"

"The judge who put my mother in jail happened to be a friend of Bob Lambert's. I'm not sure how it happened exactly. But he asked Bob and Olive if they would take me in. And they did."

Jackson would never stop feeling grateful for the opportunity to be a part of a real family. True, Olive had never warmed up to him, but the relationship he'd had with Bob and the Lambert children had more than made up for that.

"And your mother?"

"She died a couple of years into her sentence. I didn't even know she had AIDS until after the funeral."

He had regrets there. Though he'd been allowed to visit his mother, he'd still been angry at that point and had barely concealed it during the short hours they'd spent together. He wished he'd been mature enough to forgive her while she was still alive. For all her faults, she'd been kind to him always. And he knew she'd never meant to hurt him.

"Gosh, Jackson. That's so sad."

"It was a long time ago. I've had a good life with the Lamberts."

He couldn't remember the last time he'd talked about his past. Usually he sidestepped personal questions. But tonight he hadn't minded opening up to Winnie. Maybe it was the painting. It was easier to talk when you didn't feel the other person watching you. Judging you.

He ran the roller in the tray of paint, up and down, until the excess had been shed, then returned the roller to the wall. It was satisfying seeing the dull drywall take on the new, fresh color. He let his gaze slide toward Winnie who was up on the second rung of the stepladder now, painting the line where the wall met the ceiling. Her expression was earnest as she concentrated on keeping a steady hand.

Suddenly she stopped and glanced at him. "Did I mess up?"

He realized he'd been staring again. Damn. He had to stop that. "Nope. You're doing great. Have you done a lot of painting?"

"Sure. Brock and I did all the painting in the café after I bought the place. Before that, I used to help my mom paint on the farm. Not just the house, but the barn, too."

"And what was home like for you?" He'd been doing

too much of the talking. "You didn't have any brothers or sisters, did you?" At least none had shown up for the wedding that he could remember.

"I was a spoiled only child," she agreed.

No. She wasn't. Spoiled children could be self-centered and full of entitlement. Winnie was none of those things. She did have a peaceful strength about her, though, that he thought must have come from a happy, trauma-free childhood.

"I hope I haven't been boring you," he said. "Can't remember the last time I blabbed so much."

"You should blab more often. I like hearing you talk."

And maybe he'd like hearing her talk, too. "Fair is fair. It's your turn."

"But I don't have much to say. You met my mother and father at the rehearsal dinner."

The rehearsal for the wedding that never happened. "I did. Nice people."

"Yes. I was lucky." She climbed down the ladder so she could move it to a new position. When he saw what she was doing, he hastily put down his roller to help her.

While he repositioned the ladder, she stretched her neck and back, then surveyed the walls. In an hour, maybe less, they'd be done the first coat.

"It's looking good, isn't it?"

"It's an improvement," he conceded. But no amount of decorating would ever make this more than a nine-by-ten-foot room that Bobby would soon outgrow. "But not exactly your dream home, I bet."

"The days of having a dream home are far in my future." She thanked him for moving the ladder, then climbed back up to resume painting.

"If you had one…what would you want?"

"Oh, a walk-in closet. Not that I have such a big wardrobe. Still, it would be fun to have a closet with lots of space. A big tub for soaking—that would be a priority. And a bedroom and a playroom for Bobby. That's just for starters," she laughed.

He wished he could give her all that.

And more.

Damn, he was doing it again. *Keep your eyes on the paint,* he warned himself. *And your thoughts on the job.*

Chapter Six

A kid didn't get into the state foster-care program because they had great parents. Winnie understood this. Still she was stunned at how difficult Jackson's early years had been.

She found it strange that Brock had never told her the full story, but then, he hadn't talked much about any of the members of his family. At the beginning of their romance, whenever she had asked for more details about his siblings or his parents he'd just laugh, shake his head and say, "You'll meet them soon enough."

And she had. Over the months of their engagement she'd grown to know each of them a little better. B.J. she saw rarely because until he married Savannah he was almost always on the rodeo circuit. But she'd been around him enough to realize that he was the kind of guy who liked to take charge, a strong man with a good heart.

Having so many brothers who liked to tease and play practical jokes, Cassidy had learned to protect her heart. Only recently had she given it to Dan Farley, who was a real sweetheart in Winnie's opinion. Farley frequented the Cinnamon Stick Café *a lot*. He put in hundreds of miles every week as a large-animal vet and needed the caffeine to stay alert during his very long workdays.

Corb was easy to get to know because he was the most like Brock: easygoing and charming, plus, since he was Laurel's husband, she saw him the most.

It was only Jackson who had remained an enigma. Jackson who eluded her attempts to talk to him at family gatherings and who *never* patronized her café, either.

She was actually very surprised that he'd opened up so much tonight.

But there was still one subject he hadn't broached.

She dipped her paintbrush into the can, dabbed off the excess, then carefully continued along the edge of the wall avoiding making even the smallest mark on the ceiling.

"What about your dad?" She was watching her paintbrush, not Jackson, as she asked this. She suspected that not having to make eye contact with her was why Jackson was talking more than usual tonight. "Was he part of your life?"

"Nope. I've never even met him."

"So, on your birth certificate…" She'd recently filled out the form for Bobby and could picture it in her mind, especially the line where she'd had to write down the father's name. Tears had blurred her vision as she'd printed *Brock Lambert* on that page.

"My mother put *unknown* where my father's name should have gone. I always thought she was keeping his name from me, though she claimed he was just some cowboy she met at the bar one night."

Hearing the pain in his voice, she had to stop painting. So many times since Brock's accident, she'd worried what effect his death would have on their son.

Her heart ached every time she thought about it.

Just as her heart ached now for Jackson.

Because he'd grown up without a dad. Because he'd tried to take care of his mother and felt as though he'd failed. And most of all, because he felt responsible for Brock's death and the fact that Bobby didn't have a dad, either.

That was why he had spent the past week building this bedroom and now helping her with the painting.

She wondered when, if ever, he was going to feel as if his debt to her and Bobby had been paid.

She took a deep breath, then went back to something she could control—her painting.

And when she was finally done cutting in the walls, she climbed down the rungs and set her brush on the tray. "Done," she said with more fatigue than satisfaction.

"Great. I'll just move the ladder out of the way so I can get at this last section." It only took Jackson a couple of minutes and then he was finished, too.

After setting down the roller brush, he pointed at her arm. "You'll want to wash that off before it dries."

"What?" She twisted her arm, but couldn't see what he meant.

"This." Gently he took her by the wrist and rotated her forearm a few inches. With his other hand, he rubbed away a blotch of paint.

Waves of pleasure spread out from the places where he was touching her. Winnie felt the aftershocks multiplying in her body. Her heart rate zoomed; she even felt breathless.

When she looked up, for once Jackson met her gaze head-on. She marveled at the warmth in his blue eyes, the lushness of his mouth, the manly strength of his jaw and chin.

He was insanely good-looking.

How had she been so oblivious before?

"Win, don't."

"Don't what?"

"Look at me like that."

There was actual pain in his voice, but there was something else, too. Something hot and desperate. And she felt it, too.

Don't kiss him was her last coherent thought. But she was already leaning in. Closing her eyes.

God only knew what he was thinking. Or not thinking.

Because he leaned down as she leaned up, and it was happening, the thing that shouldn't happen.

They were kissing, or was it drowning?

He had his hands around her face now, holding her like a precious, wonderful thing.

And she reached out to shoulders that were so broad and strong she felt that they could carry her anywhere she wanted to go.

His lips on hers. It was like magic. To think he felt these things for her, the same things she'd begun feeling for him.

And then, it was over.

They weren't kissing anymore, not even touching. And Jackson was shaking his head, even as she was reverberating with aftershocks of pleasure.

"Damn it. I was afraid this would happen."

He stepped back from her, as if she was a dangerous, uncontrollable person and he had to be careful not to spook her.

"I don't know what it is about you," he said. "I've tried. God knows I've tried…."

Her arms dropped to her sides and hung there. They'd never felt so…empty. "I'm just a woman. An ordinary woman."

"Not to me. You were never that."

She felt as if he had her heart on a string and was playing with it. "Then why are you walking away?"

"Are you kidding me? Tell me you don't think this is wrong." Jackson's eyes, glowing with warmth a minute ago, were dark with misery now. "And while you're at it, how about explaining it to Olive, too, and the whole bloody Lambert family? And if that's not enough for you, imagine telling Bobby one day how you ended up kissing the guy who killed his father."

"Damn it, Jackson. You *didn't* kill him."

"If he were *here*. If he saw *this*." Jackson pointed from her to himself. "It *would* kill him. Trust me. It would."

What could she say to that? An ugly shame began to seep over her, staining what had momentarily felt lovely and good.

She tucked her hands into the pockets of her jeans. She felt small. Dirty. Bad.

"You better leave." She was looking at her bare feet as she said this. She'd taken off her socks so she wouldn't slip on the ladder. Now she curled her toes under. Her feet were cold. All of her felt cold.

Jackson didn't answer. But she felt his absence as he moved away from the door. She heard him exit out the front way. The sound of the door latch catching. Then the distant thud of his boots on the stairs.

THE NEXT MORNING, Winnie discovered a new universal law. It went something like this. The day you wake up grouchy because you couldn't sleep because you'd kissed your dead fiancé's brother will be the same day your normally happy little boy wakes up grouchy, too.

"What's the matter, Bobby? This is your favorite cereal, right?"

"No." He frowned at her, then pushed away the cooked-rice-and-banana cereal he usually loved.

Did he have a fever? She pulled out the thermometer to check. Normal.

Was that molar bothering him? She took a look at his gums. No sign of inflammation.

Finally she tried offering him toast with jam. Slices of apple.

These he gobbled up. Hoping he'd gone back to being her usually sunny boy, she let him play while she got ready for work. When it was time to dress him in his snowsuit and boots, he got stubborn again.

"No," he said to his snowsuit.

"No," he said to his boots.

Winnie stared at her son. "Is this national no day or something?"

He couldn't *possibly* be upset over what had happened last night, could he? He was only a toddler. He'd been in a different room. The door had been closed.

Winnie decided to phone her mother for a professional opinion. The answer wasn't encouraging.

"Bobby might be entering the terrible twos a little on the early side."

Terrible twos.

Oh, no. She hadn't read that far in her *Parenting For Dummies* book yet. And she didn't have time now.

Bobby was due at the babysitter's in ten minutes, and she had to be at the café five minutes after that.

"Do you want to ride in your new sled, Bobby?"

He looked up from the toy cars he'd been pulling from his toy chest.

It was one of the items Olive had given him in the present frenzy of two weeks ago. Winnie removed the wooden sled from the closet. She could see he was curious.

"It's an outside toy, Bobby. You have to put on your snowsuit and boots."

He eyed the sled. He eyed the boots and snowsuit lying on the floor where he'd tossed them.

Then he sighed and went to his outdoor clothes. He picked up the snowsuit and gave it to her. "Help."

A new word. He'd just said a new word. Plus, her little psychological ploy had worked. Winnie wanted to give her son a big hug and kiss, but decided it would be smarter to play it cool.

"Sure, I'll help you, Bobby. I'm glad you want to give this a try. You're going to love your new sled."

And he did. He laughed the whole way to Linda's house. The faster Winnie pulled him, the louder he laughed. *I think I've found my new workout.*

In less than five minutes Bobby was happily ensconced with his new sitter. Winnie left the sled in Linda's backyard and made it back to the café five minutes before ten.

She said hi to Vince, who was in the kitchen putting his last batch of buns in the oven. His day started early and ended shortly after lunch. Then she slipped on her apron and joined Dawn behind the counter.

The place was quiet and Dawn had her laptop open.

She wasn't working on her correspondence courses, however, but doing a little internet shopping.

"Look at these boots." She scrolled down, then clicked to enlarge the image.

"Pretty." Winnie peered at the black leather boots with stacked wedge heels. "Not very practical for Coffee Creek, though." The town only had sidewalks on a few streets. And you could never count on them being clear.

"True." Dawn sighed, then closed the laptop. "I guess I should make some fresh coffee."

"Good idea." Winnie had already noticed the pot was low and had been about to make the same suggestion. She started preparing tuna salad for that day's sandwich special and soon more customers came in and the place was hopping.

Bert from the post office showed up, like usual. He and his ex-wife were always careful not to come to the café at the same time. Winnie didn't have time to do more than give him a smile and a friendly hello.

She should have been too busy to think about anything but work.

So why did she keep having flashes from last night? The way Jackson's hand had felt on her arm.

The look in his eyes before he'd kissed her.

And then the kiss. Oh, wow, that kiss… Her knees went a little weak every time she thought about it. And him.

And she thought about both way too much. Was she going crazy?

She had to talk to someone. To Laurel. Her best friend would help her get some perspective on this.

But it was three and a half hours before Winnie had

time for a break. She ran up to her apartment, using the inside stairs, intending to call Laurel in private.

But someone was in her apartment. She could hear the floorboards creaking and the radio playing quietly, even though the connecting door from the stairs to her apartment was closed.

There was only one person who could be in there. Jackson still had the keys she'd loaned him when he'd started the project. He must have gone in the back way, as usual. Probably he was planning to be gone before she returned home at quarter past two.

Last night she'd told him she didn't need his help anymore. But she wasn't surprised that he'd ignored her. He was noble to a fault, where she was concerned.

She ought to back down the stairs quietly and let him finish the painting in peace.

But what she really wanted was to go inside and force him to talk about what had happened between them last night.

Two options. Retreat. Or advance. Which one was smarter?

Before she could decide, she felt her cell phone vibrate. Pulling it from her back pocket, she saw the call was from Laurel. She decided to take it.

"Hello?" Despite the poor soundproofing in the building, she doubted if Jackson could hear her over the sound of the radio.

"Hey, Winnie. Sorry to bother you while you're at work, but Corb just left for town and he forgot his phone. If he stops in for a coffee, would you tell him we're almost out of diapers?"

"Sure." Winnie hesitated. "Actually I was just about to call you. I need to talk about something."

"Are you and Bobby okay?"

"Yes. Well, Bobby is. Me, I'm not so sure. You're going to think this is crazy, but there's something weird going on with me and Jackson."

"What do you mean?"

"When I'm around him I feel so…strange."

"Is this about Brock's accident? Because if you're feeling angry—"

"No. I've never blamed Jackson for that. It's something else. He's been so sweet, building that extra room for Bobby. And, have you ever noticed that he's, well, he's pretty hot, actually?"

"Don't tell Corb, but yeah, I've noticed." Suddenly there was a new tension in Laurel's voice. "Hang on. You aren't saying you're *attracted* to Jackson, are you?"

Winnie didn't answer.

"He's, like, practically Brock's brother."

"I know." The words came out sounding like a groan.

"Oh, Winnie. If you think your relationship with Olive is complicated *now*. Can you imagine what would happen if—" Laurel stopped. "Wait a minute. Has something happened between the two of you?"

Oh, Lord. Should she tell her? She'd never been able to keep a secret from Laurel for long. And the temptation to talk about what had happened was very strong.

"Last night when we were painting Bobby's room… we sort of kissed."

"You didn't!"

"It was amazing. Wonderful. But also awful. After it happened I kept thinking how much it would hurt Brock if he knew…."

"It's too close to home," Laurel said. "When you talked about being ready to date again, I was so happy for you. But I never guessed you were thinking of Jackson."

"I wasn't. At least, I don't think I was."

"So...the kiss just sort of happened?"

"It sure wasn't planned. And Jackson was so upset after. He said it was a mistake."

"But you want it to happen again?" Laurel guessed.

"I do."

"Oh, Winnie. You've been through so much and you deserve to be happy. But I can't help agreeing with Jackson. It would be better if you found someone else."

Winnie had really been hoping for a different answer.

But the logical side of her had to agree.

"You're probably right. Look, I have to get back to work now. Thanks for listening." She ended the call abruptly so Laurel wouldn't guess how upset she was.

If even Laurel thought the idea was so crazy, then her attraction to Jackson really must be wrong.

She had to stop.

Thinking of him. Dreaming of him. Wanting him.

She had to stop all of it.

Winnie glanced at the door to her apartment. She wanted so badly to go inside.

Instead she headed back to the café and put on a fresh pot of coffee.

A WEEK CRAWLED BY. Winnie did her best to control her thoughts and yearnings where Jackson was concerned.

It helped that he never came into the café.

Bobby adjusted quickly to his new bedroom, but the lovely additional storage space was quickly filled to overflowing.

Had she been wrong to say no to Brock's cabin?

Thinking of the beautiful open-concept kitchen, the views of Cold Coffee Lake and the mountains beyond, the roomy two bedrooms and large mudroom—not to mention the cozy porch out front—Winnie began to think that she had.

Especially since she doubted that she was ready to start dating after all.

A few days after after her awkward phone conversation with Laurel about Jackson, Laurel and Corb had invited her to a dinner party at their home.

They'd invited several of their friends—including a horse trainer who worked at Monahan's Equestrian Center. Greg was a handsome, sandy-haired fellow with a warm smile and a great sense of humor.

She could tell right away he was interested in her, and she'd tried to be interested back. She'd even accepted and gone on a date with him last Saturday night.

It had been awful.

Excruciating.

Every time she'd smiled, she had felt like such a fake. She didn't want to be with Greg. She wanted—

Face it, she wanted what she couldn't have.

"What's wrong, Win?"

She'd stepped into the kitchen to get a fresh tray of cinnamon rolls for the counter. Vince was measuring scoops of flour into one of his large aluminum mixing bowls. He stopped and gave her a searching look.

"I'm fine."

"Three weeks ago you looked fine. Three weeks ago, I thought to myself, time has done a good job healing that girl. Motherhood must be helping. She's got her old spark back again."

Winnie sank onto a stool. Vince was rarely in a mood

to chat, and she was always glad of a chance to get off her feet for a few minutes.

"But the past couple of weeks you've looked so glum. It's got me wondering if maybe you came back to work too early."

"That's not the problem." She was definitely ready to be working again. And much as she loved and appreciated her parents, it had been time for her and Bobby to move into their own home, as well.

Vince waited. He wasn't the type to pry.

"I can't help wondering if this is it for me. Ten years from now will it still be me and Bobby living above the café in our apartment? Just the two of us?"

"And if it is?"

She sighed. "I love being a mother. But I'm not even thirty years old."

"I'd say something wise about living your life to the fullest and not being afraid of taking chances, but why should you listen to an old cowboy like me? It's not like I've made such a success with my life."

Vince had certainly done his share of taking chances—most of them on bucking bulls and broncs. He had the scars on his weathered skin and the bad knees to show for it.

"You're in the Cowboy Hall of Fame. You've beaten your addiction to alcohol. And you supply the town with the best baked goods in the state. I'd say you've had your share of accomplishments, Vince."

He nodded. "None of them was family, though. And I do have my regrets on that score." He took out a box and put a dozen buns inside. "These are for Maddie Turner. Think you could ask Jackson to come pick them up next time he's in town? The going on my bike is just too slow now with all this snow."

All it took was the mention of Jackson's name to knock her off balance. She glanced down at her hands. Told herself she could handle this.

"I'll take Maddie the buns myself, Vince. You're pretty good to her." She paused, then added, "I heard you two were once an item."

"That was a long time ago. I left her behind when I decided to become a rodeo cowboy. And that's my biggest regret. But it's not the reason I'm doing this." He folded over the top flaps, then tied the box shut with string.

"Oh?"

"Maddie's got the biggest heart of anyone I've known. Despite the way I walked out on her, she's done some real good turns for me and one very large favor. I owe her big time."

Winnie waited for him to elaborate. But Vince had already said all that he was going to on the subject.

Chapter Seven

"Is something wrong, Jackson?"

At the sound of Maddie's voice, he jumped out of the kitchen chair. "What are you doing up?"

She was in her blue housecoat as usual, shuffling in a pair of slippers that were so old her big toe poked through on the right foot. He'd tried to buy her a replacement pair, but she claimed they weren't as comfy and made him return the new ones.

"Feeling a little hungry," she said. "Thought I'd toast that last cinnamon bun."

"Go sit down. I'll bring it to you." They'd had dinner an hour ago, which she'd only pecked at. Since then he'd been going through the numbers again, preparing a financial road map for expanding the cattle operation on Silver Creek. In five years he hoped to be running seven hundred head, at least. But to get there required updating the barns, repairing fencing, resuming hay production and about a hundred other things.

"I can still operate the toaster, Jackson. I'm not that far gone." She glanced at the ledgers and spreadsheets on the oak table. The table had been in this kitchen for at least a hundred years, she'd told him, and looked like someone had beaten it with chains. "So why were you cursing? Think you've bitten off more than you can chew here?"

"Not at all." He'd only agreed to take this job after doing enough research to know he could make a success of it. "The plan is sound. I'm just having troubles with the numbers tonight. I added the same row of figures three times and came up with three different sums."

"Last time you sat down with that adding machine the two of you seemed to get along just fine." Maddie cut the remaining bun in half and slipped both sides into the toaster. Then she filled the kettle and set it on to boil.

Now that the weather was turning colder, Jackson was growing to appreciate the old-fashioned wood-burning stove and the comforting warmth it provided to the room.

"It's not the machine's fault," he admitted. He was having trouble concentrating.

And had been for the past few weeks.

Maddie sat down and looked at him thoughtfully.

"No," he said.

She laughed. "I wasn't aware that I had asked you a question."

"You had that 'do you want to talk about it' look on your face. And I don't."

"So there *is* something troubling you."

Not something. *Someone.*

"Maddie," he warned.

"Okay, okay. Consider the subject dropped." She got up to butter her toast and make the tea. As she was standing by the sink, a set of bright lights flashed through the window.

A vehicle of some sort had just pulled up to the house.

Immediately the border collies went on alert, rising from their spots—one by Jackson's chair, one by Maddie's. Usually they slept by the stove, but it had grown too warm. Once at the door, they turned back to their mistress with eager expressions.

"Who could be coming at this hour?" Maddie wondered.

According to the clock on the wall it was five minutes past seven. Not that late.

"Maybe Cassidy and Farley?" Since they'd found out about Maddie's terminal disease, all of Olive's children had decided it was time to put aside the family feud and had taken to dropping in from time to time.

Olive was the last holdout, her resentment toward her sister for past wrongs apparently something she intended to carry to the grave.

Maddie shook her head. "Cassidy's coming over tomorrow to show me her wedding and honeymoon pictures."

A wedding that Maddie, as the aunt, should have been invited to. But Maddie didn't seem to feel resentful. Jackson admired her very much for that.

A car door slammed shut. Then, about twenty seconds later, a second door. Curious, Jackson turned on the outside light. When he heard footsteps on the back landing, he opened the door.

Standing in the flood of light, with crystals of snow floating down around her, was Winnie. She had Bobby in one arm. And a bakery box in the other.

"Special delivery." She gave him a nervous smile. "Vince asked me to bring these to Maddie."

Winter brought out the best in Winnie. Her skin

glowed. Her eyes sparkled. Snowflakes settled on her dark hair and red coat like diamonds.

"Let her in already, Jackson. Good heavens, it's snowing again."

He stood aside so Winnie could cross into the kitchen. She immediately set Bobby onto his feet. The little guy's eyes were wide as he took in these strange new surroundings. He didn't look nervous, but Jackson noticed he kept a tight hold on one of his mother's legs.

"Shut the door, please." Maddie sounded a little exasperated. "Really, Jackson, you'd think we'd never had a visitor before."

He did as commanded, still feeling a little stunned.

To have a woman on your mind, all the time.

To be trying to not think of her. To be failing. And then to have her show up on the doorstep.

Glowing like the light on the top of a Christmas tree.

"Good timing. I was just making a pot of tea." Maddie crouched to the level of the toddler. "Hey there, little guy. Aren't you a cutie? I can see your daddy in you, that's for sure."

Winnie glanced at Jackson nervously. "We can't stay. Bobby usually goes to bed at eight."

He knew she was saying that for him. Explaining that she'd timed her visit specifically so she'd have an excuse to drop off the gift, then leave.

But Maddie was having none of it. "Just one cup. Look—it's already made and poured." With her too-thin hands, she carried a mug to the table. "Jackson, would you put out some of those fresh rolls to go with the tea? And a cookie for Bobby. If that's okay?"

"Bobby may have a cookie. But the cinnamon buns were meant for you, Maddie." She'd slipped off her boots and Bobby's and was now guarding the wood stove to make sure her son didn't burn himself.

She didn't have to worry. The second he spotted the dogs, Bobby fell in love. Cautiously he stepped away from his mother. He pointed and said, "Bow!" He looked up at his mom, excitement making him dance. "Bow bow!"

"Yes, Bobby. Those are dogs. And dogs say bow-*wow*." The tender look that washed over Winnie's face made Jackson's stomach do strange flip-flops.

He gripped the edge of one of the kitchen chairs, then pulled it out and nodded for Winnie to sit. "I'll watch the stove," he promised.

Trix and Honey looked from the approaching youngster to Maddie. The expression on their mugs made Jackson smile. The only other baby they'd been exposed to was Stephanie. But Stephanie wasn't walking yet.

"Stay." Maddie commanded her dogs.

So they stayed, even when Bobby got close enough to touch.

"Want me to help him?" he asked Winnie. When she nodded, he went to the little boy.

"Hold your hand like this." He closed the boy's small fingers into a fist. "And let them smell you."

Both dogs happily obliged.

"And now you can pet them. Softly." Jackson demonstrated while Bobby watched intently. A second later he mimicked Jackson's gentle pats.

"That's right," Jackson encouraged him. Winnie was sipping her tea, sitting in the chair he'd pulled up for her next to Maddie. Both women were smiling.

"Such a sweet child." Maddie placed her hand over

Winnie's. "It was so nice of you to drive all this way in this weather."

"I'm not about to let a little snow stop me from visiting one of my friends. We miss you at the café, Maddie. You were one of my best customers."

"And now I'm getting my cinnamon buns for free…."

"No, you're not. Vince pays for those."

"Oh." Maddie stared down at the table.

"I swear he's still carrying a torch for you."

Maddie drew in a breath, and that seemed to trigger one of her coughing spells. She grabbed a handful of tissues from her housecoat while Jackson jumped up and fetched her a glass of water.

Eventually the coughing subsided. She sipped the water, then apologized.

"Not at all," Winnie said. "I hope I didn't upset you by talking about Vince."

Maddie shook her head as if discounting the idea. "I'm fine, honey. Just a little tired. I think I'll go to bed now."

"Can I get you anything?" Jackson offered.

Maddie waved him back with her hand. "Just bring me my pills and water at nine."

"Will do."

Once she'd disappeared to her room on the other side of the house, Winnie apologized again.

"I shouldn't have mentioned Vince."

Jackson was still standing in front of the stove in case Bobby decided to go exploring. It didn't seem likely that he would. The toddler was following Trix and Honey from one resting spot to the other. The tired border collies were being very patient.

"She usually goes to bed around now anyway. And

she can't be too upset about Vince. She always eats his cinnamon buns." He thought about the chicken stir-fry he'd made for dinner tonight and how little she'd had of it. "They're pretty much all she does eat these days."

"You know they were an item once, before Vince got serious about the rodeo?"

He nodded. He'd heard.

"Well, today he told me that Maddie did a favor for him some time after that. He said he owed her big-time." Winnie tipped her head to one side. "Any idea what that favor might have been?"

"None. She's never talked to me about him."

He was having trouble focusing on the conversation. Just having Winnie in the same room made his thoughts go a little crazy. She brought so much life to the place.

So much beauty.

Jackson couldn't resist looking at her soft, red lips. He remembered kissing them all too well and wanted to kiss them again. Now.

God, five minutes alone with her—not counting her son, who was too young to notice—and his thoughts were already out of control.

Winnie must have sensed the direction his mind was traveling. She scrambled up from her chair, her cheeks turning as pink as they'd been when she'd first come in from the cold.

"I should get Bobby home."

"Right."

"Mind helping me with his boots?"

"Sure."

It wasn't as easy as he thought it would be. Turned out Bobby didn't want his boots on. He didn't want to go home.

"Bow, bow, bow, bow, bow..." He went on and on, repeating that one word while he flailed his arms and kicked his feet.

"You're harder to shoe than a feisty stallion," Jackson told him. "How about we switch jobs?" he suggested to Winnie. "I'll hold him and you put on the boots."

That did work better, probably because Bobby went still the moment Jackson picked him up. His large eyes studied Jackson's face, as if he was trying to make up his mind whether to like this big man or not.

But the minute Jackson passed Bobby back to his mom, he started crying again. "Down, down, down."

"Seems to really like those dogs."

"You think?" Winnie sounded tired. He could understand why. A half hour of Bobby was fun. A whole day must be exhausting.

"Let me walk you out to the car." He stepped into his boots, not bothering with a jacket. "I'll carry him."

Winnie hesitated, then passed him over.

Jackson figured the kid would start crying even louder, but again Bobby became very quiet. Looking at the little boy's rounded eyes, Jackson could see the wheels spinning as the little guy tried to figure out what was going on. Why did his mother keep passing him to this stranger?

"Time to go home, Bobby."

Winnie led the way to her car and opened the back door so he could slide Bobby into his car seat. The little boy's eyes were drooping as she buckled him in.

"It's been a long day for him. Next time maybe you could pick up the buns for Maddie when you're in town? There's too much snow for Vince to make deliveries with his bicycle anymore."

In other words, she wouldn't be coming out here again. Probably a smart decision.

"I could do that." He'd drop in early morning or later in the afternoon, when Winnie wasn't working.

She paused before getting behind the wheel. She looked a little sad suddenly.

"You okay?"

"I am. It was just so…cozy and warm in that kitchen, with Maddie, and the stove, and the dogs…"

"There's a couple of cats, too. Ginger is the friendly one. But she must have been playing shy tonight."

"Oh, I love cats. Maybe that's what I should get. The apartment's too small for a dog, but we have room for a kitten."

He considered the idea. And where it had sprung from. "Kind of lonely in that apartment of yours sometimes?"

"After Bobby goes to bed at eight… Yes, it can be. TV isn't the same as having—" She smiled ruefully. "Sorry. I didn't mean to cry on your shoulder. I have a wonderful son, great friends and a good business. Most people would say I was darned lucky."

"What happened to Brock… That wasn't lucky."

She caught her breath. "No."

"So I'd say you're entitled to the occasional sad spell."

"Thanks for understanding. I'm good now." She gave him a brave smile and a wave, then got into the driver's seat.

He stood watching as she drove down the lane, admiring her strength and bravery. If only he could be the one to comfort her. But he couldn't. Because what

Winnie really yearned for was a lover, a partner, a man who could help her raise her son.

And he could never be any of those.

WINNIE DIDN'T SLEEP WELL that night. She kept thinking back to the time she'd spent at Maddie's. The kitchen was old and outdated, with worn linoleum and ancient appliances. But it was also charming and welcoming— just like Maddie had been before Winnie had made the mistake of talking about Vince.

She wondered if she'd ever know the whole story behind Vince and Maddie's romance and friendship. But it wasn't her curiosity about their affair that was keeping her up.

No, it was Jackson. She'd loved the gentle way he'd handled her son. He'd been so protective—making sure Bobby didn't get near the stove and that the dogs were gentle and well behaved.

And every time he'd looked at her, she'd felt as if she was on an elevator that had suddenly dropped a few stories. His eyes were soulful and intense. She had trouble thinking if she looked too deeply into them.

And a few times tonight, she'd made that very mistake....

Finally Winnie fell asleep, but at three o'clock she woke from a dream. Brock had come into her room and sat on the side of her bed. It had felt absolutely real. She touched the mattress where he had sat in her dream and was almost surprised to find it cool.

"You've forgotten me, haven't you?" He'd looked so sad as he said this.

"Brock?" she'd asked, whether in her dream or real life, she didn't know. "Is it really you?"

She'd held out a hand—and he was gone.

Heart pounding, she reached for the bedside lamp and flooded the room with light.

She was alone, of course.

She sank back onto her pillow and covered her face.

The dream was a sign. She had to stop obsessing over Jackson. They'd already decided it wasn't right. It just wasn't.

AT THE CINNAMON STICK the next morning, something extraordinary happened. Watching the events unfold before her eyes, Winnie wondered if she wasn't having another dream.

Four years ago, the local librarian, Tabitha Snow, and Coffee Creek's postmaster, Burt Snow, both in their early forties, had separated, then divorced. Because neither one of them had wanted to move, and it was such a small town, they'd come up with a schedule so they wouldn't keep running into one another.

For instance, Tabitha was to buy her groceries from Molly's Market on Saturday, Tuesday and Thursday. Burt on Monday, Wednesday and Friday.

They had a schedule for Winnie's café, too. Every morning, Tabitha popped in for her blueberry muffin and coffee before opening the library while Burt regularly showed up at noon for a sandwich and a bowl of soup.

For four years this system had been working just fine.

Until now.

It was quarter to ten. Tabitha, due to be at the library in fifteen minutes, was at the counter ordering her muffin and coffee. She was a warm, unpretentious woman, with an understated sense of style. The type, Winnie thought, who would rather read an extra book on the weekend than spend an hour at the hair salon getting her gray covered.

"Just a minute," Tabitha said. "I know I have another dime in here somewhere."

Winnie held out her hand, willing the other woman to hurry. Through the front window she could see Burt. The tall, ultraslender man had just left the post office and seemed to be heading in this direction.

Maybe he wanted to check out the progress on the new historical site? The roadside tourist attraction on the other side of the highway from the café was due for an official opening later this month. Olive Lambert and Straws Monahan headed the committee that had overseen the construction of a short walking loop with informational signposts detailing the history of the area, culminating in a bronze statue of a man on a horse that was sure to be the focus of many photographs.

But no. Burt wasn't crossing the highway. He was right outside the door now. And then the bells tinkled and he was inside on the big welcome mat. And it was no mistake that he'd arrived at the same time as his ex-wife. He was looking directly at Tabitha with a marked sense of purpose.

Tabitha still hadn't seen him. "Oh, there it is. Sorry. I keep meaning to clean out my purse but—"

Winnie had opened her eyes wide, hoping to convey to Tabitha that there was someone behind her, but Tabitha hadn't noticed. Her bill paid and her breakfast in hand, she turned.

And froze.

"Hi, Tabby."

Every customer in the place went quiet, as did Dawn and Winnie.

"Hi, Burt." While the postmaster had sounded confident and strong, Tabitha's voice was uncertain and weak.

Winnie knew this couldn't be easy for her. Once, before Brock died, Winnie had gone to the library to borrow some books on planning a wedding. Tabitha had been very helpful, and they'd become friends. Weeks later, when they'd been chatting together over a cup of coffee, Tabitha had confided that her marriage had ended because Burt was too cold.

Maybe he loved me a little, Tabitha had told her. *But not enough.*

"Four years today," Burt said, his voice quieter, but not so low that Winnie couldn't hear.

Tabitha nodded.

"I was wondering if enough time had passed?" For the first time Burt looked and sounded unsure of himself. "We didn't make it as a couple. But could we be friends?"

Winnie wasn't sure how Tabitha would respond. But in the end, the librarian didn't even hesitate. "I'd like that."

Burt smiled. "Me, too."

"So...no more schedules?"

"If that's okay with you."

"Oh, it is."

Burt held the door open for her, then followed her outside. Through the window Winnie watched as they crossed the street together, chatting all the while.

Well.

She glanced at Dawn.

"Gosh," the young blonde said. "That was kind of romantic, wasn't it?"

Winnie smiled, though she disagreed; she didn't want to burst Dawn's bubble. For her, Tabitha and Burt's decision had been about acceptance and moving on.

And it made her wonder if that was the real meaning behind her dream last night. She would never forget Brock. She'd loved him and dreamed of spending a lifetime together.

That could never happen now. And after a year and half, she'd thought she'd accepted that.

But maybe the dream was trying to tell her that a piece of her was still hanging on.

Chapter Eight

Olive stopped in at the café later that afternoon, fifteen minutes before Winnie was scheduled to pick up Bobby from the sitter's. The matriarch of the Lambert family always dressed as if she managed the county's biggest and most successful cattle ranch and horse-breeding business.

Today was no exception.

Olive was protected from the cold by a lush mink coat that had been expertly tailored to mold to her slim physique. She carried a Hermès handbag, and her left hand, when she rested it casually on the counter, sported a diamond that was four times the size of the one Brock had given Winnie.

She got right down to business.

"This Thursday is a big day for the Lambert family. I want to make sure that you and Bobby will be attending both the opening of the historic landmark and Thanksgiving dinner later at the ranch."

Not so much an invitation, Winnie reflected, as a command to attend. *This must be what it felt like to be a member of the British royal family.*

But one of the reasons she'd come back to Coffee Creek was so Bobby could be close to his father's side of the family. So she resisted the urge to make a sarcastic comment and instead just nodded. "May I bring something for the dinner? A vegetable dish?"

"No need for that. Bonny's been baking and preparing casseroles all week."

Hmm. Bonny might have accepted the offer, if she'd had the chance. "How about a couple pumpkin pies?"

"Fine. Bring the pies."

Charming, Winnie thought. But she kept the smile on her face. Laurel would be proud of how agreeable she was being today.

"Would you like a coffee and a cinnamon bun for the road, Olive?"

"No, thank you. I just finished lunch. I would like to step into the kitchen and talk to—"

"No need." Vince was at the kitchen door, his immaculate white apron a contrast to his grizzled face and gray hair that looked as if he'd chopped it using a kitchen knife. And no mirror. "I'm not coming."

"But the historic landmark is commemorating the history of our town. Don't you care—"

"Never been a fan of history, Olive."

"Well, then, Thanksgiving dinner, at least. Won't you come for that?"

Winnie could tell that Olive really wanted him to say yes. And that puzzled her. Vince wasn't family. So why did Olive care?

"Is Maddie invited?"

Olive's face turned white and she pressed her lips so tightly together that they practically disappeared.

After a few moments of silence, Vince said, "I didn't think so."

Then he withdrew into his kitchen like a turtle to his shell.

The café seemed deadly quiet then.

"Sure you don't want that coffee?" Winnie offered brightly.

"Maybe I will," Olive said. "But no cinnamon bun. I'm losing my taste for them."

THE MONTANA WEATHER cooperated on the morning of the historic-landmark opening, with sunny skies and above-freezing temperatures. Winnie was relieved, because she'd decided to bring Bobby and she didn't want him exposed to an hour of blistering cold.

The ceremony was scheduled for eleven o'clock that morning. Since it was Thanksgiving, all the local businesses, including her café, were closed. Winnie settled Bobby on his sled, covering him with a blanket and giving him two of his favorite cars—one for each hand. She hoped he would be reasonably quiet and well behaved for the short ceremony.

As she pulled her son along the snow-covered road, it seemed most everybody in Coffee Creek was assembled at the crossroads of Highway 81 and Main Street.

As soon as she approached the crowd, she spotted Jackson, in a sheepskin-lined coat and a dark brown hat. He was standing near Corb, who was holding Stephanie in his arms, with Laurel standing on his other side. Beyond them were Cassidy and Dan Farley, as well as B.J. and Savannah, who were just back from their honeymoon in Australia.

Now what was she supposed to do?

She and Jackson had agreed to avoid one another. But she couldn't ignore her best friend.

Laurel had been watching for her and just that moment spotted her. She waved her blue mitten in the air. "Winnie! We're over here!"

"Okay, Bobby. I guess we don't have a choice." She pulled him toward his aunt and uncle and as soon as he spotted the familiar faces, Bobby dropped his trucks and scrambled out of his sled. But he didn't run to Corb, Laurel, or any of his other aunts and uncles. No, her son had to pick Jackson, of all people. He held out his arms and tried out his latest new word: "Up."

Jackson shot her an uncertain look.

"Do you mind holding him for a bit?" she asked.

For an answer he scooped up her son and settled him on his shoulders. Bobby squealed in delight. He'd never been carried this way before and seemed to love the view.

"Gosh. I had no idea Jackson was so good with kids." Laurel picked a grain of puffed rice from Winnie's lapel. "I love that coat on you. The red is fabulous with your dark hair and creamy skin. What's it like not to be cursed with freckles?"

Winnie gave her a hug.

"What's that for?"

"Being you." She could always count on Laurel to make her smile.

"Good morning, citizens of Coffee Creek." The mayor, Snuff McCormick, had just stepped up to the temporary wooden podium that had been constructed next to the gorgeous bronze statue of a cowboy astride an American Quarter Horse. The statue had been donated to the town over a year ago and had been the inspiration behind creating a historic landmark.

"We've gathered to open Montana's newest historic

landmark commemorating the original Coffee Creek Ranch." The burly man glanced down at his notes. "Here to explain a bit more about it is the cochair of the committee, a woman who needs no introduction in these parts, Olive Lambert."

A smattering of applause and a few cheers greeted Olive as she stepped up to the microphone. "Thank you, Snuff."

"And that's 'nuff from Snuff," Laurel whispered.

Winnie, Corb and Jackson all chuckled.

"Behave," Corb whispered to his wife. But he was still smiling as he said this.

"It must be hard for some of you younger folks to believe," Olive said, diving right into her material, "but a hundred and fifty years ago all this land stretching from our town to the boundaries of Coffee Creek ranch as it exists today belonged to the Lambert family. Since then, parcels were sold off, including the land where our town currently sits. Despite all the sales, Coffee Creek Ranch is still the largest working ranch in Bitterroot County."

There was more applause here, and Winnie couldn't help but be impressed.

It was quite a legacy. And her son was a part of it.

She glanced at Bobby. Her tow-headed, brown-eyed son was still happily ensconced on Jackson's shoulders, with a firm hold on the cowboy's thick, dark hair.

Did it hurt? Jackson's expression gave nothing away. He seemed to be giving Olive his full concentration. But then his gaze shifted and he was looking right at her. She held his eyes until she could feel the heat rising from her neck.

She tried to focus on the remainder of Olive's speech.

She caught a few snippets. Something about original ranching artifacts dating back to the mid-eighties. Something else about attracting more visitors to their charming town.

She kept her gaze fixed on Olive, but all her other senses were honed in on Jackson.

The kiss had changed everything. It was like it had created an invisible connection between them.

Now every time he shuffled his feet, or shifted his gaze, she knew.

When Olive began thanking the members of the Historical Site Committee who had worked so hard to make this dream a reality, Winnie sensed the speech was ending.

She clapped along with the others. And then Straws Monahan, with his long lanky form, was stepping up to the microphone.

Cassidy whispered in Winnie's ear, "That's my boss. He's such a nice man."

"I know him," Winnie replied. "He's one of my best customers."

"If not for Straws," B.J. commented, "half of Coffee Creek would be unemployed."

Besides providing full-service boarding for those who could afford it, the equestrian center had an eighty-thousand-square-foot indoor arena and an outdoor stadium with seating for twenty thousand people. These were used for all sorts of rodeo, riding and equestrian clinics.

Standing up on stage, Straws beamed as he thanked Olive for her tireless drive and vision. When the crowd began applauding, he clapped, too, smiling at Olive with what seemed to be genuine affection.

"Do you see the way he's looking at my mother?" Cassidy was dressed as usual in cowboy boots and jeans. A heavy suede coat protected her from the chill. She leaned her blond head between Laurel and Winnie. "Could it be he actually *likes* her?"

Corb overheard the comment. "Could be. They've both been widowed for quite a few years."

"And Straws's kids don't come home often. I heard there was some sort of fight after their mother died," Cassidy added.

B.J. frowned. "Stop all your whispering. That's our mother, and this is her big moment."

Chastened, Cassidy allowed that her brother had a point. "Let's go congratulate her."

En masse, the family worked their way through the dispersing crowd toward the stage. Somehow Jackson ended up beside Winnie, and he handed Bobby into her arms.

"Thanks for taking care of him during the ceremony." If her son hadn't been on Jackson's shoulders, Winnie was sure he would have been a bundle of activity and possibly disruptive.

"No problem. My hair probably needed a good thinning, anyway." He rubbed the top of his head and Winnie thought he was joking until she saw that her son still clutched a few strands of dark hair.

"Oh, my Lord, Bobby." She pried open his fingers and brushed away the hairs. Glancing up, she felt mortified. "I'm so sorry…"

But Jackson was laughing.

And then, suddenly, he wasn't.

Olive had moved between them, her eyes bright and her smile triumphant. "Thank you for coming, Jackson."

She actually hugged him, something Winnie had never seen her do to her foster son before.

Then she moved to Winnie and gave her a smile that was warmer and more genuine than anything Winnie had seen before, either. "I'm so glad you brought Bobby. I know he's young. But this is his heritage, too."

"Congratulations, Olive." Winnie returned the petite woman's hug. "What an exciting day."

Over the shorter woman's head, she could see Jackson withdraw. The laughter that had transformed his face only seconds ago was gone.

AFTER THE OPENING, Winnie stopped at home to feed Bobby lunch. While he was napping, she decorated the pies she'd baked last night with pastry cutouts of autumn leaves. Then she whipped some cream to use as topping, adding a tablespoon of powdered sugar, a dollop of vanilla and a sprinkling of cinnamon.

She changed into a dress that she wore with leggings and boots and used her straightening iron to control her crazy curls.

When Bobby woke up, she gave him a drink, then dressed him in one of the outfits from his grandmother. He looked so adorable in the plaid shirt and corduroy overalls that she had to take a few pictures before loading him and the pies into her little white SUV.

Coffee Creek Ranch had been decked out for Thanksgiving. Big fat pumpkins and chrysanthemums of gold, orange and dark red were arranged attractively on the front porch.

And the aromas! Even Bobby noticed. As they approached the main door—he'd insisted on walking instead of being carried, and his hand was tucked inside hers—he stopped and sniffed the air.

"Mmm." He looked up at his mother and smiled.

Winnie laughed. It seemed even when they were little, food was the way to a man's heart.

B.J. had the door open for them before they'd finished climbing the porch stairs. "Let me take that for you." He took the insulated bag with the pies and the diaper bag hanging from her other shoulder.

"Thanks, B.J."

The oldest son was also the tallest of the Lambert siblings, with dark hair, not blond, and eyes that were more gray than green.

"How was Australia?" Winnie asked. He and Savannah had returned only a day ago and she hadn't had a chance to ask either of them about their honeymoon at the opening.

"Great. We scuba dived in the ocean, rented motorbikes to cruise the shoreline and generally had a terrific adventure." He started to whisk the insulated carry case into the house.

"Careful! Those are the pumpkin pies."

B.J. raised his eyebrows and smacked his lips. "Thanks for the intel. I'll be taking these out to the—"

"Kitchen." His sister came up from behind and smacked his arm. "We all adore pumpkin pie, B.J., so you better do as you're told." Cassidy held out her arms to Bobby. "Remember Auntie Cassie? Come here, honey."

Bobby was a gregarious toddler but he'd only met Cassidy a few times, so Winnie expected him to hold back. But no sooner had Cassidy issued her invitation than, just like that, Winnie's hand was dropped and her son toddled toward his aunt.

Cassidy scooped him up and kissed his cheek.

B.J. gave his nephew a kiss, too. Then glared at his sister. "Since when do *you* order *me* around?"

Cassidy put her hands on her hips. "I've been taking lessons from your new wife. She doesn't even get her sentence out before you're jumping to do her bidding."

"Not true." B.J. pulled on his sister's ponytail as he hurried past her, presumably, *hopefully,* to deliver the pies to the kitchen.

"Brothers." Cassidy rolled her eyes.

"I used to wish I had at least one," Winnie admitted.

Cassidy looked as though she was going to say something else depreciatory, but then she stopped. Perhaps she was thinking of the brother she'd lost so recently. "They're not all bad, I guess."

"Where's your mom?"

"Actually in the kitchen." Cassidy sounded amazed, because kitchen duties were usually something Olive preferred to avoid. Then to Bobby she said, "Let's go find your cousin Stephanie. Your grandma put out some fun toys for you to play with."

And suddenly, after the commotion of her big welcome, Winnie was alone in the foyer. She hung her coat on one of the few unoccupied pegs, then took a few steps down the hall toward the dining room.

The table was set with white linens and the best china. A beautiful fall bouquet was at the center of the table, flanked with tall candles in silver holders.

In the kitchen, to her left, she could see Corb carving a twenty-pound turkey, Laurel stirring gravy on the stove and Olive pulling casserole dishes out of the oven. Looked like dinner would be served soon.

In the adjoining family room, Cassidy was on the floor playing with the toddlers. She had brought her border collie, Sky, with her, and Bobby was showing more interest in the dog than he was in the toys. Fortunately Sky, who was getting on in years, was as tolerant of the little boy as Maddie's dogs had been.

Cassidy's new husband, Farley, was chatting with B.J. by the fireplace while Savannah stood near one of the floor-to-ceiling windows, looking out at the view and having a discussion with her younger sister, Regan, who was home from med school in Washington for the holiday.

It only took an instant for Winnie to realize who was missing.

And then, suddenly, he was right in front of her.

"Good people," he said. "But overwhelming at times."

He had a beer in one hand and a glass of wine in the other. He passed her the wine and she realized he'd poured it for her. So he must have seen her drive up.

He nodded to the study on the other side of the hall from the dining room. "I was in there."

Curious to see the room she'd only ever peeked in before, she followed him inside a very masculine-looking study, with wood-paneled walls, oil paintings and several comfortable leather-covered chairs, as well as a massive desk. The window overlooked the driveway and she could see her vehicle.

"I was sitting here when you arrived." He lowered himself to one of the chairs next to the window and without thinking, she settled into the other one.

"This is peaceful."

"Yeah. It used to be Bob's office. As a kid, I loved hanging out with him in here. I'd be quiet so I wouldn't bother him. He loved reading, Westerns mostly." Jackson nodded at the bookshelves and Winnie saw an entire row devoted to the genre.

Of course, there were also books on horses, ranching and other subjects of professional interest.

"Since he passed away, this room isn't used much. But sometimes I sneak in just to soak in the ambience."

Winnie took a sip of her wine, studying the line of family photos on the shelf to her left. One photo in particular caught her eye—it had been taken along a section of fencing close to the barn. All the Lambert men were gathered in one cohesive, laughing group. At the center was Bob Lambert. She'd never met him—he'd been dead for a few years by the time she started dating Brock. But she could see that the graying rancher had a big, strong presence. He had an arm linked around Brock's neck and his other arm around Jackson's shoulders. Corb and B.J. stood behind him, both with a hand on their dad's back.

Gosh, what a handsome bunch.

But it was painful to see how carefree and young Brock looked—thank goodness he hadn't known the awful fate that awaited him.

And the smile on Jackson's face, so wide and confident. In all the time she'd known him, she'd never seen him look that happy. "Those must have been good years."

He turned to see what she was looking at. He smiled a little sadly when he spotted the picture. "Bob Lambert saved my life. And I'm not exaggerating."

He certainly looked like one of the family in that picture. Yet here he was on Thanksgiving Day, not joining the others in the kitchen and family room but holed up in Bob Lambert's office. With her.

Each of them, for different reasons, felt like an outsider.

But they couldn't hide out here all evening.

"I should offer to help in the kitchen." She got out of her chair, reluctantly, though.

Jackson stood, as well. And suddenly they were an arm's length apart, his gaze so intense she couldn't look away.

"You look beautiful tonight. I've heard some women glow when they're pregnant. Being a mother does that to you."

She could hear the emotion behind the words. And she could see desire flaming in his beautiful, soulful blue eyes.

Did he ever—

"There you are." Olive was at the door, her tone sharp, her gaze suspicious. She didn't ask what the two of them were doing in her dead husband's old office, but it was clear she was wondering.

"It's time to sit down for dinner," she added.

OFFICIAL OPINION POLL

Dear Reader,

Since you are a book enthusiast, we would like to know what you think.

Inside you will find a short Opinion Poll. Please participate in our Poll by sharing your opinion on 3 subjects that are very important to all of us.

To thank you for your participation, we would like to send you **2 FREE BOOKS** and **2 FREE GIFTS!**

Please enjoy them with our compliments.

Sincerely,

Pam Powers

For Your Reading Pleasure...

Get **2 FREE BOOKS** featuring romance the all-American way! Find love and a sense of adventure, romance and family spirit.

Free

Your **2 FREE BOOKS** have a combined cover price of $11.00 in the U.S. and $12.50 in Canada.

Peel off sticker and place by your completed Poll on the right page and you'll automatically receive **2 FREE BOOKS** and **2 FREE GIFTS** with no obligation to purchase anything!

We'll send you two wonderful surprise gifts, (worth about $10), absolutely FREE, just for trying our Harlequin® American Romance® books! Don't miss out — *MAIL THE REPLY CARD TODAY!*

YOUR OPINION POLL
THANK-YOU FREE GIFTS INCLUDE:

▶ **2 HARLEQUIN® AMERICAN ROMANCE® BOOKS**
▶ **2 LOVELY SURPRISE GIFTS**

◀ **DETACH AND MAIL CARD TODAY!** ▶

OFFICIAL OPINION POLL

YOUR OPINION COUNTS!
Please check TRUE or FALSE below to express your opinion about the following statements:

Q1 Do you believe in "true love"?

"TRUE LOVE HAPPENS ONLY ONCE IN A LIFETIME."
○ TRUE
○ FALSE

Q2 Do you think marriage has any value in today's world?

"YOU CAN BE TOTALLY COMMITTED TO SOMEONE WITHOUT BEING MARRIED."
○ TRUE
○ FALSE

Q3 What kind of books do you enjoy?

"A GREAT NOVEL MUST HAVE A HAPPY ENDING."
○ TRUE
○ FALSE

YES! I have placed my sticker in the space provided below. Please send me the **2 FREE books** and 2 FREE gifts for which I qualify. I understand that I am under no obligation to purchase anything further, as explained on the back of this card.

154/354 HDL F4XP

FIRST NAME	LAST NAME

ADDRESS

APT.#	CITY

STATE/PROV.	ZIP/POSTAL CODE

HAK-1F-10/13

Printed in the U.S.A. © 2013 HARLEQUIN ENTERPRISES LIMITED.
® and ™ are trademarks owned and used by the trademark owner and/or its licensee.

✦ HARLEQUIN® READER SERVICE—Here's How It Works:

Accepting your 2 free books and 2 free gifts (gifts valued at approximately $10.00) places you under no obligation to buy anything. You may keep the books and gifts and return the shipping statement marked "cancel." If you do not cancel, about a month later we'll send you 4 additional books and bill you just $4.74 each in the U.S. or $5.24 each in Canada. That is a savings of at least 14% off the cover price. It's quite a bargain! Shipping and handling is just 50¢ per book in the U.S. and 75¢ per book in Canada.* You may cancel at any time, but if you choose to continue, every month we'll send you 4 more books, which you may either purchase at the discount price or return to us and cancel your subscription.

*Terms and prices subject to change without notice. Prices do not include applicable taxes. Sales tax applicable in N.Y. Canadian residents will be charged applicable taxes. Offer not valid in Quebec. Books received may not be as shown. All orders subject to credit approval. Credit or debit balances in a customer's account(s) may be offset by any other outstanding balance owed by or to the customer. Please allow 4 to 6 weeks for delivery. Offer available while quantities last.

If offer card is missing write to: Harlequin Reader Service, P.O. Box 1867, Buffalo NY 14240-1867 or visit: www.ReaderService.com

BUSINESS REPLY MAIL
FIRST-CLASS MAIL   PERMIT NO. 717   BUFFALO, NY

POSTAGE WILL BE PAID BY ADDRESSEE

HARLEQUIN READER SERVICE
PO BOX 1341
BUFFALO NY 14240-8571

NO POSTAGE
NECESSARY
IF MAILED
IN THE
UNITED STATES

Chapter Nine

Winnie had the feeling that the seating plan was being scrambled, as Olive directed everyone in the family to a chair.

"No, Corb. Why don't you sit here instead?" Olive pointed to a place setting across the table from where her blond, green-eyed son was standing.

"But I thought— Oh, never mind." Good-natured as always, Corb shrugged and moved.

"Now, Jackson, you can have that chair." Olive pointed to the place that Corb had just vacated.

Winnie was given the seat to Corb's right. Which meant that, if Olive hadn't interfered, she'd have been sitting next to Jackson. Was she paranoid for suspecting that Olive had deliberately separated them?

The harvest feast on the table was bountiful and aromatic. Each dish—from the golden roast turkey to the pecan-studded yams—was beautifully presented on Olive's cream-colored platters and casserole dishes.

There were mashed turnips and carrots, cornmeal dressing with hazelnuts, whipped garlic-rosemary potatoes, lightly buttered brussels sprouts and beets with a ginger-orange glaze.

Olive was supervising her grandchildren, so for a

change Winnie could enjoy her meal without worrying about how much Bobby was eating.

Winnie tasted a little of everything.

Conversation waned as everyone savored the amazing dishes Bonny had prepared for them. Only Olive wasn't focused on the food. She was enjoying her grandchildren much too much for that.

As she speared a piece of tender turkey from the platter, Winnie noticed Corb raise his wineglass in private tribute to Laurel who was across the table from him. Laurel gave her husband a cheeky wink before sipping from her own glass in response.

A few minutes later Winnie spotted B.J. feeding his new wife a piece of a brussels sprout. "Bonny has a special way of cooking them."

Savannah took the brussels sprout into her mouth.

"Delicious, right?"

"Mmm-hmm." But Savannah was looking at B.J., not the vegetable.

A moment after that, Cassidy said something so quietly only Farley could hear.

"Stop it, Cass. You are unbelievably bad." But he was fighting a grin as he said this. And then he kissed the tip of Cassidy's nose.

These quiet, loving moments between the couples at the table made Winnie smile.

They also made her heart ache.

Stop feeling sorry for yourself. You have Brock's son. You have your business...

But her gaze went to Jackson, who was eating his meal like it was a job that needed to be done. Was he impervious to all the romantic vibes around them?

Winnie sighed.

Half an hour later, so much food had been eaten, it seemed her pies would go to waste. But everyone had saved just enough room for one slice of pumpkin pie and a cup of coffee.

"Absolutely delicious, Win," Laurel gave her a thumbs-up from across the table. "What's the secret?"

"I blend a cup of ricotta cheese in with the pumpkin."

Several people asked for her recipe, including Laurel and Savannah's sister, Regan.

Then it was time to clear the table and do dishes. Winnie was happy to help, especially since Olive was still anxious to spend time with Bobby and Stephanie. She'd bought them a few presents, and once they were unwrapped, she took the toddlers and their new toys into the bedroom she'd transformed into a play area for her grandchildren.

"I don't think Corb and I will ever need to buy Stephanie a single gift," Laurel said softly, so only Winnie could hear.

"Olive's generosity is...overwhelming."

"That's one way of putting it." Laurel rolled her eyes.

Corb had turned on the television after dinner, and now most everyone was settling in to watch some football. He grabbed his wife around the waist, then pulled her down beside him on the sofa.

Next to them were B.J. and Savannah.

Farley and Cassidy were sharing the loveseat.

And Regan was on the floor, texting her boyfriend.

Jeez. Winnie hung back in the kitchen. She'd never felt like such a third wheel. Where had Jackson slipped off to?

She checked Bob Lambert's office. He wasn't there.

On an impulse she slipped on her jacket. Snow had helpfully dusted the yard and she could see a set of fresh cowboy-boot tracks leading to the barn the Lamberts called the home barn. It was the oldest barn on the property and was used to house the horses the family used for riding and moving cattle.

Winnie went through a gate, then headed for the sliding doors. As she grew close, she could hear Keith Urban singing "Raining on Sunday." Must be the radio.

But the song, about spending a stolen day under the covers with a special someone, made her heart feel heavy again. A moment later she realized Jackson was singing along and a thick, sweet yearning came over her.

Jackson had a good voice.

The barn door was open a crack, and she slid it along the track to make a space big enough for her to slip through. Jackson was in one of the stalls, going over a beautiful red bay with a currycomb. He had his back to her, but he must have heard her coming because he stopped singing.

"This is Red Rover. She was my horse when I lived here and worked for the ranch."

"She's beautiful." They both were. The cowboy *and* his horse. Winnie put a hand on Red Rover's back as she slipped into the stall next to Jackson.

"Yeah. She has great cattle sense, too. Corb said I could take her with me when I left, but I didn't feel right about that. I miss her, though."

The sadness in his voice was almost more than she could stand. She knew it was more than missing his horse.

It was missing the father who had never been part of

his life, and the mother who had died far too young. It was the guilt surrounding Brock's death and the feeling that no matter how hard he tried, he would never really belong on Coffee Creek Ranch.

It was a strong man with a tender heart trying not to let anyone see the pain within....

"Jackson..." She put her hand on his shoulder and felt the solid muscle underneath. Her heart surged with the need to show him how much she cared.

"Stop," he said. "You should go back in the house."

"Why?" Because he was feeling vulnerable? But that was exactly why the timing was right. "I know we agreed to forget about our kiss. But I can't."

"Winnie..." He said her name like a warning.

"Please, Jackson. I need to talk about what happened."

He didn't ask what she meant, but she could feel him take a really big gulp of air. Then he set down the currycomb and led her out of the stall.

"I haven't been able to forget, either," he admitted.

Suddenly her nerve faltered and she almost ran from the barn. But then she nodded. "Everything changed after that night. At least for me. I can't look at you without wanting..." Her voice lowered to a whisper. "Without wanting you to kiss me again."

His eyes widened when she said that. Then he shook his head. "You're just feeling lonely. I saw you looking around the Thanksgiving table. All those happy couples. It's hard to be alone, Winnie. I get that. But it doesn't mean you and I should...do anything rash."

"I'm not just trying to fill a void."

"Are you sure?"

She put her hands on her hips. "Single guys come

into my café every day. And two weeks ago, Corb and
Laurel set me up with one of their friends."

"They did? With who?"

"It doesn't matter who. Because I didn't feel anything. I even went out for dinner with him."

"You did?"

Jackson's two-word sentences were becoming almost comical. But Winnie could tell he was genuinely
bothered.

Which was good.

It proved that he was feeling the same way that she
was.

"The dinner was a flop. There was a man on my
mind the entire time and it wasn't my date."

Jackson's eyes traveled from her eyes to her mouth,
then back to her eyes. She felt as though he was looking
for something. Something she wanted to give.

"You can't deny we have a connection." She took a
risk and moved a step closer to him. "Jackson?"

He made a sound, almost like a desperate groan.
"You're making this so hard, Win."

"It doesn't have to be."

He swore, a blunt word that had her eyes flying wide
open.

And the next second he was kissing her. Almost
sweeping her off her feet. She needed his arms to steady
her, because she was lost now. Nothing mattered but
him. Jackson Stone. Who wanted her as desperately as
she wanted him.

"I don't believe this."

The voice didn't seem like it could be real. But it
sliced through the heated moment like a cold knife
through warm butter. With Jackson's arms still hold-

ing her close, Winnie turned to see Olive framed in the opening by the barn door.

"I wondered why you two kept sneaking off together. Now I know."

FOR SEVENTEEN YEARS Jackson had lived at Coffee Creek Ranch knowing Olive barely tolerated him and had only agreed to be his foster parent because her husband had insisted. Jackson had done his best to stay out of her way, to work hard and earn his keep and to avoid trouble at all costs.

But she'd never stopped treating him like an outsider. Even when he was in charge of the quarter-horse operation, she'd never granted him signing authority over the ranch account, the way she had with Corb, B.J., Brock and Cassidy.

If a job went wrong, if money was missing, hell, if an animal got sick—she found a way to blame him.

And he'd endured it all while he was under her roof.

But he was his own man now.

And he had reached his limit with her interfering ways.

Especially since she was targeting Winnie now, too.

"We were hardly sneaking, Olive. I came out to say hello to my horse. And Winnie needed some fresh air." He squared off against Olive, his stance solid and confident, one hand still on the small of Winnie's back.

"Don't you lie to me, young man. I saw what you two were up to."

"You mean the fact that we were kissing? We're both single. We have nothing to apologize for." He kept his voice calm yet firm, hiding his own feelings of doubt and guilt about the situation.

Winnie looked at him, as if amazed that he was remaining so composed.

"This is disgusting." Olive's tone was blistering. "We treated you like a member of our family. Now I find you sneaking off to the barn to kiss Brock's fiancée."

God, the woman knew how to press his buttons. He waited a second for the heat of his anger to taper. "We didn't sneak out. We came openly. And the kiss—not that it's any of your business—just happened." Jackson glanced at Red Rover, then back to Olive. "I understand that this is your property. I should have asked your permission before coming out here."

"Don't be ridiculous."

He inclined his head, acknowledging this. "Then let me ask the same of you. I accept you have the right to restrict where I go on your property. But no right at all to tell me who I can kiss."

He could tell his efforts to stay calm and rational were having the opposite reaction on Olive. Her eyes were brilliant green, her face red, her lips tight. Pressure was building up in her like steam from a kettle under the heat.

"I'd like to know what Brock would say about this." Her voice was full of indignation. "If he only knew…"

In a flash of anger—that she would bring this up, that she would stoop so low—Jackson spoke without thinking. "But Brock doesn't know. And he can't. Because he's gone."

Olive gasped at his blunt words and Winnie touched his sleeve as if to restrain him. She looked shocked and confused.

And why wouldn't she? He'd told her that he considered a relationship between the two of them inappropriate. Now here he was, defending their kiss to Brock's mother.

Olive planted her hands on her hips. "I guess you're right, Jackson. I can't tell you what to do. But let's just say I'm extremely disappointed." She narrowed her eyes at Winnie. "With both of you."

No sooner had Olive left the barn than Red Rover's tail went up and a patty of poop plopped out.

Jackson patted his horse. "Couldn't have said it better myself."

Winnie laughed, a nervous, forced sound. "That was awful. I shouldn't have followed you out here." She covered her face with her hands. "I can just imagine what she's going to tell all the others when she gets back in the house."

"I bet she says nothing." Jackson suspected Olive would stay silent, hoping her condemnation would stop their budding relationship from going any further. "But either way, it isn't her business. This is between you and me."

"Maybe. But as Bobby's grandmother and an important citizen of this community, Olive has the power to make both of our lives miserable."

"That's true. But I'm sick of being pushed around and manipulated by that woman." He took a deep breath. "We should go out tomorrow night, Win. Just the two of us."

She looked at him dubiously. "I'd like that. But are you sure it's a good idea?"

He wasn't. But damn it. A man could only take so much. "These past couple of weeks, trying to avoid you and not think about you... They've been hell."

"For me, too," she said softly. "But it's the Thanksgiving weekend. Might be hard to find a sitter."

He'd never dated a single mom before. This was going to be complicated. But before he could come up with a plan B, she had one.

"How about you come over to my place for dinner?"

He was about to say yes when he realized that wasn't fair to Maddie. She'd hired him to be more than a ranch foreman. He was supposed to be providing her with care and companionship, as well. If he went out tomorrow, that would make two meals she'd spent on her own over the Thanksgiving weekend.

So he made a counter offer. "Why don't you let me cook for you? Would you and Bobby like to come out to Silver Creek?"

"Seriously? You'll cook?"

"Sure. If you bring another one of those pies. I'm thinking of Maddie, of course."

She laughed.

It was a real laugh this time, and the tight ball of tension in his gut finally loosened. He felt a smile break out on his face.

"It's a deal." She glanced toward the house. "Should we head in now?"

"You go ahead. I'll finish up with Red Rover. It would be diplomatic if we didn't enter the house together."

She nodded her agreement. "So Bobby and I will see you tomorrow?"

"Yup. Around five good?"

She agreed, then slipped out the door. He resisted the urge to watch as she walked away. Instead he focused on his horse, finishing the rubdown that Winnie had interrupted earlier.

In the wake of Winnie's departure it seemed as if a warm glow lingered in the barn. But slowly the warmth faded and he was left realizing that he'd been so determined to defy Olive, he'd gone against his own better judgment.

Could he really date Winnie without feeling guilty about Brock?

He didn't know.

But it seemed he was going to give it a try.

"What gives with you and Jackson?"

Laurel was in the passenger seat of Winnie's SUV. It was Black Friday and they were on their way to Lewistown to do some shopping. They'd left Bobby and Stephanie napping at Laurel's place, with Corb in charge. He'd been sitting on the sofa with a bag of chips and a soda watching football when they'd left.

Winnie suspected he'd be a lot less relaxed when they returned.

In years gone by, Black Friday had meant a chance to shop for fashions and early Christmas gifts. Today, she and Laurel were on the hunt for bargains on diapers and baby clothes.

"Sorry to be blunt," Laurel added. "But I've been dying to ask you."

"I give you credit for waiting this long."

"I was hoping you'd bring it up first."

Laurel's voice was slightly reproachful, and for good reason. They didn't normally keep secrets from one another.

"Let me ask you something first. What did Olive say yesterday when she came in from the barn?"

"She said she had a headache. Then she went into her room and slammed the door shut."

"That's it? She didn't say anything about…"

Laurel sighed. "She didn't need to. The chemistry between you and Jackson yesterday was pretty obvious. The way you hung out together in the study before dinner. Then stared at one another all during the meal."

"We didn't stare." She glanced at her friend and noted the raised eyebrows. "We *didn't*."

"Watch out for the cow."

"What?"

"Watch out for the cow!"

Winnie was already on the brakes at that point. Fortunately the road was dry and the car stopped without skidding. The black Angus cow standing in the dead center of the road gave her a bored look.

"Go!" Winnie waved her hand. "Shoo." She tried honking her horn, and the cow, after some thoughtful deliberation, finally moved a few feet over so she could pass.

"Stupid cow." Winnie focused on the road as she brought the car back up to speed.

"So?" Laurel asked. "You were saying…"

She could see she had no choice. "I know you told me it would be weird if Jackson and I had a thing. But I've tried not to feel that way about him, and Lord knows he's tried not to feel that way about me, but—"

"You can't fight it anymore?" Laurel suggested.

"That's right. We can't." She took a deep breath, then risked a quick look at her friend. "Is this going to be a problem?"

"Not for Corb and me." Laurel was quick to reassure her. "I didn't realize your feelings were already so strong or I never would have tried to talk you out of it."

"Really? Oh, Laurel, I'm so relieved to hear that. We're having our first official date tonight. What do you think B.J. and Cassidy will say?"

"I'm pretty sure they'll be cool with it, too. But Olive is another matter."

"I know," Winnie said glumly. Any other woman and she wouldn't be too worried. But this was Olive. And for better or worse, she was still Bobby's grandmother.

Chapter Ten

To say Corb was desperate to hand off responsibility for the babies when Winnie and Laurel returned from their shopping trip might have been stretching the truth.

But not much.

He was standing at the door to the cabin when they got out of Winnie's car. He had on his boots and jacket and was just putting his hat on his head.

"Hi, honey." He kissed Laurel, then nodded at Winnie. "Kids are inside. I need to check on the cattle."

And he was gone.

Laurel and Winnie exchanged a look, then laughed. Winnie grabbed one of Laurel's two shopping bags, then followed her friend inside. As Corb had promised, Stephanie and Bobby were right there, on the floor in the foyer. Stephanie gnawing on a large plastic horse and Bobby trying to wrest it away from her.

"Hey, Bobby. Leave Stephanie's toy alone. Did you miss Mommy?" Winnie grasped him firmly under the arms, then whirled him in the air, the way he loved. Bobby giggled and forgot about the plastic horse.

"That was fun." Laurel set the packages on the wooden bench, then picked up her daughter. "But it's good to be home."

Winnie checked the time. All day long, the prospect of her evening with Jackson had been simmering in the back of her mind. Now it was time to go. She checked her hair and makeup in the powder room, then gave Stephanie a kiss and Laurel a hug before dressing Bobby in his jacket and boots.

"Have fun," Laurel said, but Winnie could see the hint of worry in her eyes. Her friend was doing her best to be supportive, but she still had reservations about the wisdom of Winnie dating Brock's foster brother.

To be fair, so did Winnie.

She'd baked a pumpkin pie that morning, and it was chilling in a covered cardboard box in the trunk of her car. Fortunately, the Montana weather was hovering above the freezing point, which meant the pie shouldn't be frozen when they went to cut into it later that evening.

It took ten minutes to drive to Silver Creek Ranch. At this time of day the sun was already very low in the sky and the dusting of snow on the ponderosa pines made every vista look like a Christmas card.

Even the ranch house and outbuildings on Silver Creek—most of which were in need of some repair or at least a fresh coat of paint—looked beautiful when frosted with snow in the fading light. Smoke hung in billowing clouds over the chimney, and once Winnie had parked and stepped out of her SUV, she could smell the scent of hickory in the air. Something else, too. Roast beef?

"Hey there." Jackson appeared at the door. Dark hair almost falling over one eye, a shadow of a beard covering his chin and jaw, he made her heart stop, then start with a happy skip.

They didn't kiss hello. It was too soon for that.

But when Jackson smiled, she could feel, right down to her fingertips and toes, how happy he was to see her.

He came out to help, taking Bobby from the car seat then grabbing the diaper bag with his other hand. She rescued the pie from the trunk and followed him into the house.

Maddie was waiting, seated at the kitchen table, her lovely eyes sparkling when she saw them. "We're celebrating Thanksgiving a day late," she told them. "And with prime rib rather than turkey."

"Sounds delish."

"It will be," Jackson promised. After making sure Bobby was well out of the way, he opened the oven and pulled out a succulent-looking roast, studded with herbs and garlic. "My special recipe," he said with a grin at her and Maddie.

"There is something about a man at work in the kitchen…" Winnie was reminded of Vince, who, though decades older than Jackson, also managed to cook without compromising a shred of his masculinity.

"A winning combination," Maddie agreed.

Winnie had brought toys for Bobby, but he ended up being much more entertained by petting and pulling on the ears of the dogs at Maddie's feet.

Watching him, the older woman's smile went from delighted to sad.

"It's so lovely to think that this beautiful child is Brock's son. But it makes me regret that I never told Brock how much I appreciated his help. He used to come round every month or so, you know." She glanced at Winnie as she said this.

"Yes. He told me the feud between you and his mother was...horse manure."

Maddie laughed and Jackson, who was making gravy on the wood-burning stove, chuckled, too. "I think Brock would have been a little more direct."

"He was," Winnie admitted. "But you shouldn't worry, Maddie. He knew you appreciated his efforts."

"I'm glad. But I still say one should never put off saying the things that need to be said." Maddie rubbed her thumb over a ring that she wore on her little finger. It was the only jewelry she wore, Winnie noted, though the older woman had made an effort with her appearance for the evening.

She was wearing a beautiful wool sweater, the same vivid green as her eyes. And she'd put on a little blush and mascara.

Maddie would never be pretty, like her sister.

But she was attractive. And when she smiled, you could sense her inner goodness.

"You and Olive are so different," Winnie found herself saying. "It's hard to believe you're sisters."

"I inherited my looks from our father, while Olive took after our mother. But I wonder what she looks like now? I haven't seen my sister, except from a distance, in several decades."

"What was it that came between you?" Winnie couldn't resist asking. According to Laurel, Olive resented Maddie for not letting her be by their father's side on his deathbed. But it just seemed so unbelievable that Maddie could be so cruel.

"Olive blamed me for keeping her from our father. But the truth was, Dad never warmed to Olive." Maddie rubbed her ring again. "I suspect he blamed Olive for our mother's death. Though he would never admit it, he always favored me over her."

"So Olive resented you for that?"

"For good reason. I lapped up my father's affection. Not until I was much older did I understand how hard it must have been for Olive. I've always wished there was some way to make amends. But Olive won't talk to me. Years ago I tried writing letters. But they were always returned. I've given up on the idea of a reconciliation. But our feud… It is my life's biggest regret."

The room fell silent. It seemed to Winnie that after all these years, most people would be willing to put the past behind them. But Olive wasn't most people. The same determination and drive that had made her such a success in the ranching business was not conducive to mending fences with her sister.

Jackson served dinner a few minutes later and Winnie enjoyed every bite, from the tender roast to the deliciously flavored gravy, roasted squash and steamed broccoli. Jackson had even baked Yorkshire pudding that was light and flavorful, as good as the ones Winnie's own mother made at home.

So he was gorgeous.

And he could cook.

Why was this terrific man still available? As far as she knew, he'd never even had a serious girlfriend.

"Why are you giving me that look?" Jackson had been watching Maddie, making sure she ate her food and didn't just move it from one pile on her plate to the other. Now his eyes were on Winnie, narrowing suspiciously.

"Just wondering where the flaws are."

"Huh?"

Maddie knew what she was talking about though. She patted Winnie's hand. "Speak to me later. I'll tell you."

Terribly curious, Winnie had no choice but to put the subject aside, and for a while they discussed Jackson's plans for expanding the ranch that spring.

Fifteen minutes later Bobby's head was drooping.

"I should take him home."

"Couldn't he sleep here for a while?" Jackson asked quickly. "I haven't given you the tour yet."

She didn't want to leave so soon, either. She and Jackson hadn't had a minute alone.

And she was still hoping to talk to Maddie, as well.

So she agreed to settle Bobby down on some cushions in the sitting room. To be safe, Maddie suggested they let the dogs outside. "It's not that cold, and they could use a little outdoor romp."

"How about we put on our coats and take a tour of the barn at the same time?" Jackson suggested.

So they left Maddie on the reclining chair where she could keep an eye on Bobby, and with the dogs on their heels went out into the cool November evening.

"It's a beautiful night. Look at those stars." She was nervous. She had to work to draw in a breath.

Jackson took her hand in his and gave it a tight squeeze. "Thanks for being here. Maddie was so excited when I told her you and Bobby were coming for dinner."

"Really?"

"Yes. She takes all the blame for the rift between her and her sister. But when you compare their lives, it doesn't seem fair. Olive had a long, happy marriage, and four healthy children. She's made a success of her ranch, too."

"While Maddie has ended up sick and alone…"

"With the ranch almost at the point of bankruptcy," Jackson added.

"She's lucky to have you."

"Some would say I'm the one taking advantage of her." Jackson opened the door to the barn, then pulled on a string to turn on the light.

Winnie looked around at the roughly constructed stalls and lack of amenities. The differences between this and the high tech facilities on Coffee Creek Ranch were enormous.

"Why do you say you're taking advantage?"

"Because she's planning to leave me everything. The house and barns aren't worth that much. But Maddie still owns a lot of land."

"I guess it's her prerogative to give the land to whomever she wants."

"She can. But I plan on giving half of it back to the Lamberts."

"Would Maddie want that?"

He hesitated. "I can't keep it all. I'm not family."

That bothered him, she realized. A lot. "After your mother died, did Bob Lambert ever consider adopting you?"

She could see a light spark in Jackson's eyes and guessed that this had been a dream of his once.

"He asked me if I'd like that. I said yes. The truth was, I was desperate for him to make my place in the family legal. Even though I had lived fifteen years as Jackson Stone by then, I would have gladly taken the Lambert name, as well."

"Why didn't it happen?" Winnie asked, but then realized she knew the answer. "Olive blocked it."

Jackson nodded slowly.

"Why would she be so nasty?"

"You can't blame her. She was protecting the things she loves the most. Her land. And her children."

He was right. That was what Olive cared about.

But not Jackson. He had only been a kid, looking for a place to belong.

And maybe nothing had changed. Maybe he was still searching for those things, even though he was now an adult. She thought about how often Jackson hung back on the perimeter of things like family gatherings, and even at the ceremony for the new historical site.

Not once could she remember him taking center stage at anything. Even a conversation.

"And now for the real reason I dragged you out here." Jackson moved closer, pulling her into his arms.

"So you could kiss me?" she teased.

"Oh, yeah." And then he did just that, but the kiss they shared this time was different. Not so much about passion and exploration, but sweeter.

Slower.

Tender and caring.

His lips lingered on hers for a long, long time. Then he swept a kiss over her cheek, her forehead, the tip of her nose.

"I could get addicted to this," he whispered in her ear.

She already was.

THEY DIDN'T DARE linger in the barn for long, and once they were back inside the house, Maddie told Jackson she needed a few minutes with Winnie. "For some girl talk."

He couldn't get out of the room fast enough when he heard that.

Winnie perched on a footstool next to Maddie's chair. She could see her son from here, too. Bobby looked so peaceful when he slept. So innocent and pure.

"Jackson is a catch, dear. But he won't be easy to hold." Maddie's tone was frank, but kind. "I don't want you to be hurt. You've had enough of that for one lifetime."

The older woman took her right hand and touched the ring that Winnie still wore. "For a relationship to work, you have to give everything. But Jackson is a man who is used to holding back."

Winnie nodded, understanding that she was right, and feeling a cold frisson of fear working under her skin.

"We have a strong connection," she said.

"I can see that. And it's a good start." Maddie didn't say anything more. But Winnie knew what she was thinking. *It wouldn't be enough.*

But Maddie's advice was coming too late. She couldn't pull back now.

And maybe Maddie would be wrong. Jackson might be ready to change. For the right woman.

Bobby let out a whimper then. Maybe he'd had a dream. Or felt a draft. At any rate, it seemed a sign that they should be going.

"Thanks for a lovely evening, Maddie. I hope we'll see you again soon." She checked Bobby's diaper and decided it was dry enough to make it home.

"I hope so, too. Good night, dear."

In the kitchen, Jackson held Bobby so she could put on her own coat and boots.

"We should talk to Olive," she said quietly. "See if she would come and visit Maddie before it's too late."

"B.J. already talked to her about it. She said no."

Winnie raised her eyebrows.

"You want me to try again?"

"Don't you think it's the right thing? If it would give Maddie some peace?"

Jackson cupped her face with his hands. "You are seriously complicating my life, Winnie Hays."

Didn't she know it.

And it worked both ways.

THE FARMHOUSE WAS always quiet after Maddie went to bed for the night. Jackson didn't like to turn on the TV in case the sound bothered her. Normally he read.

But tonight he was restless. He'd already cleaned the kitchen to a state of spotlessness that might well be a new record for him.

He'd asked Winnie to text him when she arrived home so he'd know she'd made the trip safely. She had. Two hours ago. And still he kept looking at his phone, hoping she'd send him another message.

So this was what it was like to be crazy about a woman. He'd always wondered.

For some reason, it had never happened to him before. Oh, he liked women just fine, but he tended to look for them in bars and at rodeos and to hook up for fun, never seriously. At the end of the evening, he sure didn't wonder what she was doing. Or thinking. And when he would see her again.

But tonight he was wondering all three of those things about Winnie.

He paced the length of the house, from the kitchen through the dining room to the sitting area, over and over. He wished he could go outside for a walk, but he was worried Maddie might call him for more pills or have a coughing jag and need him. At her last appointment, she'd found out the cancer had spread from her lungs to her bones.

She'd turned down the offer of more treatment to minimize her discomfort.

"All I want now is to die at home on my ranch," she'd said. And as long as her pain remained manageable, she would get her wish. How long she had, no one knew.

Could be weeks. Could be months, according to the oncologist.

Jackson didn't like thinking about when those final days would happen or what they'd be like. And he sure as hell didn't want to imagine the farmhouse without Maddie.

He still had no idea why she was insisting on leaving this ranch to him. When she'd first presented her offer, she'd told him there were reasons. And he'd find out in time.

But how much time would it take?

And could he ever feel comfortable accepting such an incredibly generous gift?

Turning the ranch around, investing his own savings, being here for her during her last days—none of that seemed like enough payment to him. Certainly not the being here part—that he would have given free.

No one should die alone, the way his mother had.

The sound of coyotes yipping in the distance took

him to the window. The dogs sleeping in Maddie's room didn't raise a fuss, fortunately. But he turned off the lights in the house, trying to see if he could spot them.

He couldn't.

But their howling raised the hairs on the back of his neck.

His mother had died alone, but Maddie wouldn't. He'd be here. But he wasn't the person she really wanted.

Maddie wanted to make peace with her sister. That wasn't likely to happen. But Winnie thought he should give it another shot.

Deep in his gut, Jackson recognized it was the right thing to do. But he didn't like his chances of succeeding.

Chapter Eleven

Jackson is a man who is used to holding back. Maddie's words played through Winnie's head all that night and led to a very restless sleep. She appreciated that the older woman was trying to protect her.

But Maddie had never been married. So she wasn't exactly an expert.

The text message Winnie received from Jackson when she woke the next morning was reassuring.

Good morning, beautiful.

Just the fact that he was thinking about her made her feel warm and happy. Then later he sent another message. Taking your advice and talking to Olive today. Wish me luck.

Fingers crossed, she responded. Toes, too.

JACKSON SMILED AS he read the text message from Winnie. He'd just finished his chores and was now cooking hot cereal for Maddie's breakfast. She liked it with warm milk and applesauce.

He was spooning the cereal into a bowl when another message arrived.

You're a good guy. Thank you.

He wasn't so sure that he was, but he was glad his decision had pleased her.

He carried a tray with the cereal and a weak cup of tea into Maddie's bedroom. The dogs had come out with him earlier when he'd gone to the barn, and now they were sleeping again. Ginger the cat was here, too, curled up at the foot of Maddie's bed.

"A woman could get used to this service." Maddie pushed herself to a sitting position so he could set the tray on her lap.

Next he opened her curtains. Thank God there was a lot of sunshine in Montana. The long winter months would be depressing without it.

"How'd you sleep?"

"Fine."

She always said the same thing, though he suspected it wasn't true. The wadded tissues strewn around her nightstand spoke of a restless night and more of the infernal coughing. He'd told her to call him—just press the intercom button on the phone by her bed—and he'd be here. But she'd have to be at death's door before she disturbed him. It was the stoic rancher in her.

"I've decided to talk to Olive today," he announced. "I'm going to invite her over for tea."

Maddie reached out and touched his arm. "Thank you."

The gratitude in her eyes made his own grow suddenly moist. "Got any tips on how I should approach her?"

"As a matter of fact, I do."

JACKSON WAS VERY familiar with Olive's schedule. She did little hands-on work at the ranch anymore—except when it came time to move the cattle in the spring and the fall. Those were trips she seldom missed.

For the most part, though, Olive focused on management and administration. She began every morning by touring the barns and speaking to Corb—who was the foreman of the cattle operation—and B.J.—who oversaw the quarter-horse breeding business.

Afterward she returned to the house for a hearty breakfast, and then the rest of the day she divided between business calls and trolling the web for any good horse sales.

Jackson timed his visit for shortly after breakfast, and it was five minutes past ten when he knocked at the front door. Bonny Platter, the housekeeper and cook, answered.

"What are you doing knocking?" she scolded him. "Come on in."

"I don't live or work here anymore," he reminded her.

"So? You're still part of the family."

Was he? Jackson seriously doubted if that would be Olive's view. "Is Olive around?"

"In the kitchen," Olive's voice carried from the other room.

Bonny shrugged, then gestured for him to follow.

Olive was dressed in wool trousers and an expensive-looking sweater. Her hair was nicely styled and she was wearing makeup and her pearls. He guessed she had a meeting in town later that day.

For now she was settled on a stool at the large granite-covered island. She had her laptop open in front of her and was making notes. Or she had been. She set down her pen.

"Jackson." She gave him a slight nod. "This is unexpected."

He'd considered phoning first, but had decided the element of surprise might work in his favor. At least this way she couldn't avoid him.

With his hat in his hands, he took a stance. "I'm here to pass along a request."

"Bonny," Olive said, not taking her gaze off him. "Maybe you could clean the bathrooms this morning."

Taking the hint, Bonny left the room.

"So. What is your request?"

Olive spoke with a frosty tone that Jackson was very familiar with. In the past that voice had made him quake with fear. But he wasn't a kid any longer.

"The request is from Maddie. Your sister."

Olive blinked once, then twice. "I know who Maddie is, thank you."

"And you also know she's sick?"

"Dying of cancer, you mean?"

Taken aback by her callous tone, he nodded. "She'd like to see you. So I'm here to invite you to tea. Any day that's good for you."

"Really? Any day that's good for me?" She let out a laugh of disbelief. "Let me tell you something, Jackson. When it comes to Maddie Turner, no day is good for me. You've been part of this family long enough that you should know this."

"I was hoping you would reconsider. Given that the situation has changed."

"And what change are you referring to? The fact that you work for Maddie now, that you're actually going to inherit my family land from her? Or is it the new situation between you and Winnie, the woman who was once about to marry my son? There are so many *changes* with you these days, Jackson, I can't keep them all straight."

Oh, but she was angry. He could feel the snap and pop in her eyes as she glared at him.

Maybe Maddie would have been smarter to send her request via Corb.

But she'd asked him to do it. So had Winnie. And now he was here. He'd just have to state his case and hope for the best.

"I'm sure you have your reasons for not wanting to go. But Maddie does have something that she'd like to pass on to you. In person."

Olive's eyes widened. She thought for a minute, then asked quietly, "What is it?"

He hesitated, then said, exactly as Maddie had asked him to, "Something of your mother's."

"So you were out at Maddie Turner's place last night?" Vince asked. He was about to punch down the dough for his second batch of cinnamon buns.

Winnie made fists with her hands. She yearned to sink them into the soft cloud of yeasty-smelling dough.

But when he'd first come to work at the Cinnamon Stick, Vince had made it clear. No one messed around in his kitchen except him.

So she resisted.

And considered his question. "Bobby and I were invited for dinner. We're going tonight, too. Would you like to join us?"

She and Jackson had been exchanging text messages all day. The last one had been another invite to dinner.

She'd said yes.

Of course she'd said yes.

She could hardly wait to see him again. And she knew Bobby would be happy to go back to the ranch and see the "bows." She still hadn't convinced him to call them dogs.

"That wouldn't be a good idea."

"Why? You could deliver a batch of your baking in person for a change."

He just shook his head as he continued to knead the soft dough.

"I don't understand. You said Maddie had been a good friend to you."

"True. Best way I can repay that is by keeping my distance."

"Are you sure? She's asked to see Olive. Maybe she'd like to see you, as well."

"Did she really?" He gave a vicious twist to the dough. "Olive will turn her down."

"According to the text message Jackson sent me an hour ago, Olive has agreed to go to tea at Silver Creek Ranch next week."

"You don't say." Vince shook his head. "I knew it was a cold start to winter this year. But I never guessed hell had frozen over."

THE MORNING WENT by slowly after Winnie's conversation with Vince. There were no more text messages from Jackson. He must have gotten busy.

But that didn't stop her from hoping he'd drop by the café to say hello.

Did he think of her as much as she thought of him? It was hard to tell.

At one-thirty in the afternoon, Cassidy came in for a large takeout coffee.

The pretty blonde was wearing a tawny-colored suede jacket that emphasized her green eyes, as well as the remnants of the tan from her honeymoon in Maui.

"Straws wants me to drive out to the Parnell ranch, about an hour east from here. They're having trouble loading one of their horses in their trailer." Cassidy chatted as she waited for Winnie to ring in her coffee. "They think their horse was traumatized in some way and want me to work with him."

"So Straws has you making house calls now? Or should I say, horse calls?"

Cassidy laughed. She looked happy and contented. Taking a job at the Monahan Equestrian Center had been good for her, Winnie reflected. Even though it meant not utilizing the accounting degree she'd worked so hard for.

Her marriage to Dan Farley wasn't hurting, either. The strong, manly vet provided good counterbalance for Cassidy's soft heart and spirited nature.

Winnie passed over the takeout mug that Cassidy had carried in with her. "Have a safe drive, Cass."

"I will." She started for the door, then stopped. Lowering her voice, so the customers sitting at the back couldn't hear, she said, "Just so you know, I'm rooting for you and Jackson. So are Corb and B.J. We know Mom is bound to give you a hard time. But just remember, not all the Lamberts think the way she does."

"I appreciate you saying that."

"Not that it isn't going to take some getting used to. I mean—Brock and Jackson. They're so different."

She knew what Cassidy meant.

Brock had been an open book. He loved to talk and could be counted on to speak his mind. He was also very charming and often said the sweetest things.

Jackson was none of those things. He was reserved and quiet: a man of action, not words. Of course, with Jackson, the compliments might be rare, but he delivered them with such single-minded intensity that they felt genuine and sincere.

Stop it.

She shouldn't compare the two men. It wouldn't be fair to the memory she wanted to preserve of Brock. Or the future she hoped to build with Jackson.

"Look at that." Cassidy pointed to the window, where a truck that was unmistakably Jackson's was slowly cruising by. "Speak of the devil."

Winnie smiled. She'd just been wishing he would come by. And here he was.

But minutes passed without Jackson coming into the café. Cassidy left and a new customer came in. Once she'd taken care of them, Winnie moved to the window, where she glanced down Main Street. She could see Jackson's truck parked outside Molly's Market.

As she watched, he emerged with several bags of groceries, which he loaded into the truck.

Surely he'd come and see her now?

But when it became clear that he was planning to drive by, she ran out to the street, gasping at the cold air and almost skidding as the clogs she wore to work made contact with the icy sidewalk.

"Jackson!" She waved an arm, but he was already pulling over to the curb and lowering his passenger window.

"What's wrong?" He had a hand on his door in case he needed to spring to her aid.

She wrapped her arms around her ribcage. "Nothing. I just thought you'd stop in."

"No time. I picked up some supplies for dinner tonight, though. See you then?"

She tried not to feel disappointed. It was silly when she was going to see him again in just a few hours.

THAT EVENING, after Maddie had retired to her room and Bobby had fallen asleep again on a quilt in the sitting room, Jackson took hold of Winnie's hands.

They were sitting on the sofa and had just finished a game of cribbage, which they'd started earlier when Maddie was in the room with them.

Now, finally, they had a little privacy.

She gazed into Jackson's eyes and marveled at the intense desire she saw in them. These were eyes she could never tire of looking into. She wanted to touch the side of his handsome face and feel his sensuous lips press against hers.

He brushed a strand of hair back from her eye, letting this thumb linger on her cheek. "It's real nice of you to bring Bobby out here to spend the evening with Maddie and me."

"I'm happy to do it."

He stroked the side of her face, then took hold of her hand again. "But it's not exactly a date, is it?"

"Not exactly."

She sighed. Between her responsibilities as a mother to a young toddler and his duties to care for Maddie in the late stage of cancer, they were each left with precious little time to be alone.

Being alone *together* seemed even more rare.

Not that she would ever begrudge the evenings he spent with Maddie. Some—like Olive—might accuse him of buttering up the older woman so he could inherit the ranch, but Winnie knew better.

Jackson treated Maddie with genuine respect and caring.

Even before she'd offered him her ranch, he'd put new roofs on her house and the cattle barn.

No, she didn't question his motives.

But she did wonder how she and Bobby might fit in the picture.

If, indeed, Jackson intended them to fit at all.

"I've done a little arranging," Jackson said. "I hope you don't mind. Corb and Laurel have agreed to take Bobby for the evening tomorrow. And B.J. and Savannah are going to come here to have dinner with Maddie. Which means you and I are going to have some time on our hands."

She smiled. *Yes.* This was exactly what they needed. "Time is good."

"The question is, what to do with it? Would you like to go to a movie in Lewistown? Or maybe out for dinner at the Green Veranda?"

What she really wanted was to be alone, *all* alone, with Jackson.

But she didn't dare say that. "Dinner sounds nice."

Besides, her apartment was conveniently just a block away from the restaurant....

JACKSON COULDN'T DENY the nervous feeling in his gut as he prepared for his date with Winnie the next evening.

Did he want to spend the evening alone with her?

Hell, yes.

But he was honest enough to admit that he hadn't yet mastered the guilt he felt whenever he thought about the fact that Winnie was supposed to be *Brock's* bride.

He and Brock had grown extremely close during the years he'd spent at Coffee Creek Ranch. While B.J. had been initially suspicious and perhaps even jealous of the new kid his father had taken in, both Corb and Brock had been open and friendly from the start.

Corb had been a few years older, though, and so it had been Brock to whom he'd gravitated during the few hours of leisure they had each day.

As the younger son, Brock had enjoyed having someone to teach for a change, and he'd quickly passed along a myriad of ranching skills to the green city kid.

They'd made a good team and, recognizing this, Bob Lambert had often assigned them tasks to work on together.

As adults, they'd both ended up focusing on the quarter-horse operation, leaving Bob and Corb to deal with the cattle and hay farming.

Then Bob had died, and Corb had become the lead man on the cattle end.

After Brock's death, Jackson had similarly stepped in to manage the quarter-horse operation, until last summer when B.J. had quit the rodeo and come home to settle down with Savannah.

By then, Jackson had been more than happy to step away from his position and take the opportunity offered to him by Maddie Turner. Even if Maddie hadn't made her offer, he'd been ready to leave and would have taken the first foreman job that came his way.

While Coffee Creek Ranch had been a great place to work, it hadn't felt right once Brock was gone.

Jackson knew he'd always miss him.

But did that also mean he'd always feel guilty for falling in love with Brock's woman?

He appreciated the fact that the Lambert kids had all made a point of telling him they had no objection to the relationship. But none of that really mattered if he couldn't feel right about it in his bones.

Jackson glanced at his reflection in the mirror on the back of his door.

He'd dressed in his best dark jeans and a black shirt with silver trim, fresh from the cleaners. Which meant it had actually been pressed, something he never bothered to do with his working clothes.

He'd gone to all this effort because Winnie was worth it. He wanted her to be proud to be seen with him. And he wanted this evening—the first they had ever spent alone as a couple—to be a success.

The lingering guilt he felt about Brock... That was going to lessen with time.

Jackson drove to town, where he picked up a bouquet of red roses from Molly's Market before presenting himself at her door, exactly at the time he'd said he'd pick her up.

It took her a while to come to the door.

He started to wonder if something had gone wrong.

But Corb had sent him a text—Just picked up Bobby. Have a great time!—and had attached a smiling face to the end of the message.

That had been an hour ago. So what could be the problem?

And then, finally, the door opened and Winnie was

on the other side. She looked gorgeous, with her dark hair falling in lovely curls over her shoulders, wearing a dress the same color as the flowers he'd bought because she looked so damn good in red.

He knew he should say something. But words failed him. He thrust the bouquet at her, feeling as awkward as a teenager on his first date.

"Sorry. I'm not good at this." He couldn't even remember the last time he'd had a real date, one where he picked the woman up at her home instead of late at night in the bar.

"The flowers are lovely. Let me put them in water."

He waited as she pulled a vase from a cupboard over the stove. Her dress made the most of her curves, even though it covered a fair amount of her skin. She was wearing dark tights with the dress and boots made of expensive leather that clung to her long, slender legs.

He had a primal urge to rip it all off her. The dress. The leggings. The boots.

He glanced down at the tips of his own boots—which he'd cleaned and polished just a half hour ago. Took a deep breath. He was here to woo her. Not ravish her.

He had to remember that.

But it turned out he wasn't any good at wooing.

Conversation over dinner was awkward. Winnie did her best. Apparently her parents were enjoying their first winter in Arizona.

Jackson couldn't have cared less.

All he could think about was how Winnie's eyes sparkled when she talked, how easily she smiled and how the curved neckline of her dress revealed a tantalizing glimpse of cleavage....

She was just as sunny and beautiful on the inside,

too. She could have her pick of single men. Not just in the county, but probably all of Montana.

So why would she choose him?

He wasn't charming like Brock. And he was no way near as wealthy as Brock had been, either.

Sure, he stood to inherit some land, but it would take years before Silver Creek could turn a profit. And it might not. He might fail and lose everything—not just the inheritance, but his own savings, which he'd pumped into the place.

When the waiter offered dessert, he wasn't surprised Winnie refused.

She obviously couldn't wait for this "date" to end.

On the walk back to her apartment, she linked her hand through his arm. "Is something bothering you?"

He didn't answer at first. He waited until he'd delivered her back to the safety of her building. And that was when he told her.

"I guess our experiment failed."

"It did?"

"Don't tell me you enjoyed that?"

"Not even a minute of it," she admitted.

At least she was honest.

He stared down at the tips of his boots again. Somehow he'd managed to scuff them during the short walk to and from the restaurant. They no longer looked shiny and new.

He sighed. "Well. Olive will be happy."

"What about you? How do you feel?"

Her question surprised him. He glanced up at her face and was shocked to see tears gathering in her eyes.

"I feel like I botched the most important night of

my life. I tried to do it by the book. But I'm not a dinner and roses guy."

"Did I ever *say* that was what I wanted?"

"No. But that's what *all* women want, isn't it? Flowers and romantic dinners in nice restaurants…"

"Oh, Jackson." She shrugged off her coat, letting it fall to the floor. "Why have we wasted the past two hours?"

Chapter Twelve

Jackson had seemed like a stranger up until that moment. As soon as Winnie flung off her coat, though, the tension snapped. He picked it up and hung it on the hook next to the door.

"Take care of this coat. I'm partial to the way you look in red." He put an arm around her waist and looked at her with more appetite than she'd seen in him all evening.

"So you like my dress?"

"Love the dress," he murmured. And then he kissed her.

Long and thoroughly.

When he was done, he pulled away a few inches. "Hello, Win."

She smiled, understanding that he was asking for a fresh start. "Hey there, cowboy."

"One good thing about tonight. At least now you know I'm the kind of guy who would rather cook my woman a meal than take her out to a fancy restaurant."

Winnie tried not to smile. The local Green Veranda wouldn't meet many people's definition of "fancy." But she understood what he was saying. "I wouldn't be living in Coffee Creek if I wanted big-city life, Jackson.

I'm as country as they come. One day I'll take you to meet my folks, and when you see the farm where I grew up, you'll understand."

"Let's do that. As soon as your folks come back from Arizona."

So he *had* been listening to her during their dinner. He'd looked so uncomfortable she hadn't been sure.

"Want to watch a movie?" she offered.

"I'd rather just sit next to you and talk." He ran his hand down her arm and her skin sparkled to life with just that simple touch.

"Sounds good. Can I get you something to drink? Wine or a beer?"

"How about I make us a cowboy coffee? I still owe you dessert."

"If by cowboy coffee you mean coffee boiled over a campfire, no thanks."

He looked amused. "I've had plenty of those. And no, I wouldn't dream of making you that. My personal recipe is in another class all together. That is, if you have fresh cream, cinnamon and brandy?"

"All of the above." She pulled out the ingredients and watched while he made a pot of decaf in her coffee press, then heated the cream and swirled in the brandy and cinnamon.

"Okay. This is pretty darn good." They were sitting on the sofa by then. Jackson had his arm around her and she was leaning against his chest.

"Tell me more about growing up on your farm. Did you have pets?"

"Oh, yes, I did." Jackson was stroking her hair, which felt lovely. "We had our dog, Gruff, and a cat Mom named Cash, because she loved Johnny Cash. Oh, and a chicken, too."

"A chicken?"

"You have a problem with chickens?"

"Hard to house train?" he suggested.

"Mom didn't let her step inside the door. June used to follow me around the yard and I'd feed her special treats."

"June? As in Johnny Cash's wife?"

"Mom's idea, again. I used to hide June's eggs so Mom couldn't find them. I couldn't stand the idea of eating June's potential babies."

"Sounds like you had a lot of fun growing up on your farm."

"I did." He sounded wistful, and she thought of what he'd told her about his childhood. A lot of it had sounded hard. Moving from city to city. Never knowing his dad. There must be some happy memories, too. At least, she hoped. "What about you? Did you have any pets?"

"Not when I was living with my mom. It was all she could do to take care of me. Once I moved out to Coffee Creek, all I wanted was a horse. Never told anyone, of course. It seemed like way too much to ask for. But after I'd been living on the ranch for a year, Bob took me to a horse sale and when I spotted Red Rover, well, I knew she was the horse for me."

"Sorta like love at first sight?"

"No. That only happened to me once." He set down his coffee, and hers, as well. Then he kissed her again.

And kept kissing, until something got them talking once more. They spent hours cuddled on the couch that way. Intimate conversation punctuated with kisses that were carefully controlled so no lines were crossed.

Every now and then, though, Winnie would catch a heated look in Jackson's eyes. He was holding back tonight. And that was probably wise.

But part of her wished he would just let go.

JACKSON LEFT WINNIE'S apartment after midnight. He'd wanted to stay the night and was pretty sure Winnie would have let him. But he didn't want to botch this by moving too fast.

He couldn't remember ever enjoying a couple of hours more than the ones he'd just spent with her. As soon as he'd driven out of town, he rolled down the window of his truck. He didn't care about the cold winter wind. His heart was on fire and he needed to feel the fresh air against his face.

He cranked up the radio and sang along with the country tune that was playing, happy that it had a fast beat and a catchy melody. You could always count on Keith Urban for both.

The feeling of euphoria didn't last long, though. All it took was coming upon the curve in the road, and the plain white cross that marked the spot where they'd hit the moose and Brock had died, to make him sober up.

Forgive me, Brock. For being the driver when you died. For loving your girl. For living even though you can't.

A WEEK LATER, Jackson prepared the farmhouse for the visit from Olive. First he swept the floors and washed the countertops. Then he put the kettle on to boil. Earlier Winnie and Bobby had driven out to pitch in. Winnie understood how important this visit was to Maddie and she wanted to help make it go as smoothly as possible.

He appreciated her thoughtfulness, especially since he'd been a little withdrawn since their date.

In his head he knew that Brock wouldn't want Winnie to grieve forever. Nor would he want his son to grow up without a father. It was just taking his heart a little longer to make the adjustment.

But it would happen eventually. It had to.

Because he couldn't imagine living without Winnie in his life.

"They're here," Winnie called out. She was standing by the kitchen window and he went to join her.

Laurel had told Winnie that Olive would be showing up with B.J. and Corb, as well as Cassidy, for moral support. Now Jackson watched as the four of them emerged from the white SUV that Olive normally drove.

B.J. had been the driver today, though, and he ran to the passenger door to take his mother's arm and lead her along the shoveled path to the kitchen door.

Maddie had insisted that he not shovel the other path, the one that led to the front door, because *Family comes in the back.*

Maddie had been on edge all day. She'd taken a shower and dressed carefully in the same nice sweater she'd worn for Thanksgiving.

She'd also made cookies, which had been an effort for her. More than once he'd seen her stop to take a rest. But when he offered to help, she shooed him away.

"This is from a secret family recipe. You can't watch."

"You'll give me your home and all your land, but not your secret recipe for cookies?" he teased.

Maddie laughed, but she still wouldn't tell him the recipe.

Then Winnie and Bobby had arrived, early, the way he'd asked them to. He felt that Maddie would appreciate the support.

And frankly any excuse to spend time with Winnie was good by him.

"Ready, Maddie?" he asked.

"Been waiting decades for this day. Let them in. It's cold outside."

And it was. A cold front had blown down from the Arctic a day ago, bringing temperatures that hurt the lungs if you inhaled too deeply. That cold air crept in with the Lamberts as they filed into the Turners' homey kitchen. Last in was Corb, who shut the door quickly behind himself. But still Jackson could feel the infusion of cold air as it swirled around the kitchen and then settled at their feet.

"Add some more wood to the fire, would you, Jackson?" Maddie, sitting in the chair at the far end of the table, smiled at her guests. "Welcome. All of you. And thanks for coming."

B.J., Corb and Cassidy all stepped forward to give their aunt a hug, but Olive lingered near the door, only taking a seat when B.J. brought one of the chairs and placed it right there on the welcome mat.

Though she was trying to be circumspect, Jackson could see Olive studying the room, as well as her sister. A few times her lips trembled, but then she'd press them together. And regain control.

"Tea is ready," Winnie announced. She filled delicate teacups that were completely at odds with the serviceable brown teapot.

For the first five minutes the younger generation dominated the conversation. But eventually Maddie cut through the nervous chatter.

"It's good to see you here, Olive."

"I don't know why."

"We grew up here. I remember helping you do your homework at this very table." Maddie fingered one of the grooves in the oak. "I believe you did this when you were struggling with algebra."

"That's past. It's your kitchen now. It's been yours for a long time."

Maddie stifled a cough. "I'm sorry for how hard things were for you growing up. Dad took Mother's death so hard. It changed him. I don't think he meant to be so hard on you—"

"Stop." Olive's voice was commanding, her eyes bright with a determined glint. "I didn't come to hear you justify the way you ingratiated yourself with our father, even going so far as to keep me from him during his last days on earth. You said you had something for me. Something of Mother's," she added, her voice a touch softer.

"Yes. I found this after Dad died." Maddie began working a ring off her baby finger. "I wanted to give it to you sooner, but—"

She didn't finish her sentence. She didn't need to, Jackson thought. Everyone in this room knew Olive would never have taken a call or accepted a visit from Maddie.

"This was our mother's wedding ring." Maddie glanced at the small diamond ring one last time before passing it to Cassidy, who was seated next to her on the right.

Cassidy studied the ring, then passed it to Corb, who handed it to his mom.

"I often wonder how different our lives would have been had she lived," Maddie said softly.

But Olive wasn't listening. She was holding the ring in her hand as if it was a priceless artifact. The harsh light in her eyes had softened. Even the corners of her mouth were curving upward marginally.

Maddie had worn the ring on the baby finger of her right hand, and it had taken some effort to remove, even though she'd lost quite a bit of weight lately.

Olive, however, slipped the ring easily onto her fourth finger.

It fit perfectly.

Everyone had said Olive took after her mother. Apparently they were right.

After a few seconds had passed, Olive finally addressed her sister. "Thank you. I'm very glad you decided to give me this ring rather than hand it over to Jackson, the way you're doing with the rest of our heritage."

"Oh, Olive."

Maddie must have been hoping the gift of their mother's ring would work a miracle on Olive. But clearly it hadn't changed a thing. Before their eyes Maddie seemed to deflate. The gray circles under her eyes became more pronounced. Her cheeks sunk even deeper.

"It's time to go." Olive stood. She glanced at her children, expecting they would all do the same.

But they weren't even looking at her. Their eyes were on their aunt.

"I never wanted to come between you and Dad." The words were a quiet plea, but Olive couldn't accept it.

"I'm sorry that you're sick, Maddie. But we can't change the past. B.J., are you coming or not?"

"Not, Mom." Her eldest son passed her the car keys. "We were invited for tea. And we're staying for tea. I'm sure Savannah won't mind picking us up and giving us a lift home."

Only B.J. would have the nerve to talk to his mother this way, Jackson thought. Well, Cassidy might, too. She was obviously firmly in support of her older brother. Only soft-hearted Corb was clearly torn. In the end he opted to stay, but only after walking his mom to the car and seeing her safely on her way.

Once her younger sister was gone, Maddie gave in to a coughing spell that went on for at least a minute. As usual, Jackson got her a glass of water, wishing there was something more helpful that he could do. He could see concern displayed on all the Lamberts' faces as they sat helplessly, waiting for the fit to pass.

And eventually it did. Maddie drank her water, then sank deeper into her chair and closed her eyes. "I should have known nothing would change."

"Why didn't you tell Olive the truth?" Jackson asked. "You didn't keep her from your father's deathbed. He didn't want her there. She blames you for that, but it isn't fair."

"I could never tell her that. It would only confirm what she's always known but never been able to accept. Our father didn't love her. It's awful. But it's true."

"That is awful. But so is how Mom treated you. Especially today." Cassidy stomped one of her feet against the planked floor. "All she wanted was that stupid ring."

"Don't be too quick to judge," Maddie cautioned. "You grew up with two parents who loved you. Can you imagine what it would be like to have no mother—because she'd died giving birth to you? And to have a father who hated you for that very reason?"

Jackson figured he was closer to being able to imagine that scenario than any of the Lamberts, or Winnie. But at least he'd had his mother when he was younger.

It seemed that Olive had had no one. Except the sister she wouldn't let herself love.

HALF AN HOUR later, Savannah drove up in her sheriff's SUV and collected B.J., Corb and Cassidy. Maddie was sleeping in her reclining chair in the sitting room, with Bobby napping on the quilt nearby.

It had been an eventful afternoon.

Winnie rinsed another teacup, then handed it to Jackson to dry. "Lord knows," she finally said, "I'm not a big fan of Olive's. But I think I'm starting to feel sorry for her."

"I know what you mean."

"On the other hand, Laurel grew up in sort of a similar situation. Her mom died of cancer when she was a little girl and it broke her dad's heart. He never really wanted Laurel after that, and she knew it. That's why she spent so much time at our place."

"You'd never guess to know her. She's got such a great sense of humor and she's so upbeat." Jackson opened a cupboard and started putting away the fancy cups. On a top shelf, Winnie noticed. Who knew when they'd be used again?

When Maddie died? Oh, Lord, what a depressing thought.

"Exactly," she said. "A person can overcome a tough

childhood. But it also makes you realize how much can be lost if you hang on to old resentments and regrets."

"Is this segueing into a lecture on my behalf?" Jackson teased.

She turned her head so he wouldn't see her guilty flush. "We haven't talked about Brock for a while. I'm hoping it means you've finally put the accident behind you. Have the nightmares stopped?"

"You worry too much. We wouldn't be having this relationship if I was still hung up about Brock's death." He pulled her away from the sink and into his arms, where they enjoyed a nice, leisurely kiss.

But when it ended, Winnie pulled back to study his eyes. As usual, they were guarded.

He hadn't actually *said* that the nightmares were over.

But she wouldn't push him.

It had been a good week, she reflected. She and Bobby had spent almost every evening here at Silver Creek Ranch. And on Sunday Jackson had promised to take them out to find a couple Christmas trees. A small one for the apartment and something grander for the farmhouse.

They had two reasons for wanting to make it a special Christmas this year. One reason was Maddie. It seemed very likely that this would be her last Christmas.

Whereas for Bobby, who had been born in early January, this would be his first.

Winnie didn't want the holiday to be just an orgy of opening presents. She hoped to instill in her son the importance of family and traditions…and helping others who were less fortunate. Which was why she wanted to take him with her next week when she delivered home-baked Christmas cookies to the Mountain View Care Home.

He might be too young to get the message now. But over the course of many years, she hoped it would sink in.

"You're awfully thoughtful," Jackson commented.

"I was just thinking about Christmas. I want it to be perfect this year."

She expected him to agree. But instead he looked concerned. "Don't set your sights too high."

She wanted to ask him what he meant by that. But Bobby chose that moment to wake up.

"Mama?"

Not wanting him to bother Maddie, she rushed to the other room.

ON SUNDAY, WINNIE stepped out of her car into six inches of fresh snow. "Good thing I wore my boots, Bobby Boy."

"Boots!" he echoed happily, kicking his own against his car seat as he waited for her to release him. "Snow!" he said next, when she set him down so she could grab the picnic she'd packed for their Christmas-tree-hunting expedition.

"Hey there!" Jackson emerged from the house with a down parka, hat and gloves. "Talk about a winter wonderland."

Winnie almost said, *It's perfect,* but stopped herself. It still bothered her that Jackson had warned her not to set her sights too high the other day.

As if he knew that something was going to go wrong.

Well, it wasn't.

"Here, I'll take this little guy." Jackson leaned over to scoop up Bobby, who squealed with excitement. "And that." With his other hand he snagged the insulated bag with the picnic snacks inside.

Then he kissed her, softly on the lips, then the nose. "How did you get so cold already?"

Instead of answering, she tried to make a snowball to throw at him, but the dry fluffy crystals flew away in the breeze and he just laughed at her.

"So I've hitched a couple of Maddie's horses to a sleigh I found in the back of the tractor barn." Jackson led the way around a grove of aspen trees, with their slender white trunks and graceful bare branches, to the fenced-in pasture that surrounded the cattle barn.

Out front was the team of white draft horses, snorting in the cold. Jackson had combed out their manes and tails and tied red bows to the harness so they looked show ready.

"Wow, Jackson. They're beautiful."

"Aren't they? Maddie fell in love with them and paid a pretty penny."

"I thought she was strapped for money."

"Yes. And it's because of decisions like this. She thinks too much with her heart." Jackson placed the insulated bag in the sleigh, then took Bobby to say hi to the horses and feed them each a chunk of carrot. "The former owners had a sense of humor. They named them Thelma and Louise."

Winnie had watched the movie with her mom years ago. "You expect me to let my son ride in a sleigh with a suicidal duo like that?"

But she was already climbing into her seat, excited to get started.

Jackson settled Bobby on her lap before getting into the driver's seat. As soon as they started moving, Bobby began clapping his hands and didn't stop.

"Cow! Cow!" he kept insisting, pointing to the horses and smiling with glee.

"His dad must be rolling over in his grave," Jackson said.

Winnie just laughed. She wasn't in the mood to correct her son. He'd learn soon enough, and right now he was just so darn cute.

They returned to the ranch an hour and a half later, having found what Winnie considered to be two excellent trees, though Jackson insisted they both could be stand-ins for *A Charlie Brown Christmas*.

"Wait until they're decorated," Winnie insisted.

Jackson carried the bigger tree into the house and set it into the stand to thaw while Winnie warmed up soup and made sandwiches for lunch.

After they'd eaten, Maddie directed them up to the attic, where several boxes of old ornaments and lights were moldering. Jackson wiped off most of the dust before carrying them down the ladder, then spent the next five minutes sneezing.

Digging into the old boxes was like discovering lost treasure. Winnie found old-fashioned strands of lights, colorful glass balls and garlands for the windows.

"These are priceless!"

While Bobby and Maddie napped, Jackson helped her decorate the tree. They strung the lights first, after checking that they still worked, then added garlands.

"Now the ornaments," Winnie said, handing one to Jackson to place at the top of the tree.

"Decorating the tree is more work than cutting it

down." Jackson's tone was mild, though, as he made the protest.

"You've done this before, I take it," Winnie said, noting how careful he was not to group similar-colored balls together.

"Olive is a stickler about her Christmas trees. They have to be perfect."

"And when you were younger, living with your mom. Did you have Christmas trees then?"

He paused. "I don't think so. Not that I remember."

"But you *did* celebrate Christmas?"

"Most years we exchanged gifts."

Which implied there had been years when they didn't.

"Christmas wasn't a big deal to us."

"Really?" She didn't know many little kids who didn't love Christmas.

"Really," Jackson insisted. "If Mom was sober, I was happy. It was all I ever wanted. I do remember one year we went to Mom's parents for Christmas dinner. The food was good, but the tension between my grandparents and mother was awful. They were fighting before we made it to dessert. I was so glad to get out of there."

"They weren't nice people?"

"At the time, I was totally on my mother's side. Now that I'm older, I get where my grandparents were coming from. They wanted Mom and me to move in with them. They wanted to pay for her to go back to school. It was all good stuff, but back then I believed my mom when she said they were just trying to control her."

"Oh, gosh, Jackson." She felt so lucky in comparison, but it really wasn't fair. Why did some children have so much and others so little?

"Hey. Don't feel sorry for me. It wasn't that bad. At least, not until Mom hooked up with that last boyfriend of hers. But let's stop talking about that. It's almost dark. Why don't we turn out the lights and see how the tree looks?"

Winnie kicked aside the last empty box and went to the switch on the wall. Just as she turned out the lights, Maddie came out of her room and gasped with pleasure.

"Oh, my. That's lovely."

And it really was.

Energized by the proceedings, Maddie went to the kitchen and added some cinnamon and cloves to her homemade apple cider, heating it on the stove until the entire house smelled like Christmas.

When it was ready, Jackson poured the cider into large mugs and the three of them sat down to admire the tree. Winnie set her mug on a coffee table, then picked up her sleepy son and cuddled him close in her arms.

Maddie sighed with pleasure. "This house hasn't been decorated for Christmas since my mother died. This brings back so many memories.... Thank you both."

Winnie was stunned into silence by the disclosure. She glanced at Jackson and saw an equally shocked look in his eyes.

That meant Maddie hadn't celebrated Christmas since she was a very little girl. And Olive had grown up without ever decorating a tree or hanging a stocking for Santa.

The more she learned about Olive's past, the more sympathy she felt for the older woman. No wonder she clung to her own children with a ferocity that was almost desperate at times.

Chapter Thirteen

That evening, it started snowing again and Jackson and Maddie both tried to talk Winnie into spending the night.

"I can't. I don't have enough diapers for Bobby."

"I could drive into town and buy some," Jackson offered.

Winnie laughed. "Don't be silly. We'll be fine."

Acquiescing reluctantly, Jackson helped her out to the car. It took a few minutes to figure out how to work the infernal car seat, but he eventually had Bobby buckled in.

"You should own a truck. Not that dinky car," he told Winnie as he held the driver side door open for her.

"It's an SUV," she insisted of her little white Toyota RAV4.

"A *baby* SUV," he insisted, "is not as good as a truck. We can't even fit your tree in here."

He was nervous about leaving Maddie home alone, but even more nervous about Winnie driving in what was turning out to be a blizzard. "Sure you won't reconsider and stay the night?"

"I really can't. Diapers aren't an option for Bobby at this age. Trust me."

She was laughing at him, he realized. But he was determined to get the last word. "Okay, then. I'm driving behind you to make sure you get home safely. That way I can bring your tree, too."

"But you can't leave Maddie alone."

"I'll phone Corb. Have him on standby in case anything goes wrong." He went back inside to call Corb and explain the situation, then he told Maddie that if she needed anything at all, she was to phone Corb. He could be at Silver Creek in ten minutes.

"I'll be fine," Maddie insisted. "I've got my water and my pills. And after such an exciting day, I'm sure I'll sleep well tonight."

It was satisfying to know she'd enjoyed the day so much.

Decorating for the holidays wasn't really his thing. But hanging out with Winnie and her son was.

Then again, he figured he could muck out a barn with Winnie and still feel like he'd had a good day.

He made sure the phone was within easy reach of the bed, then checked the food and water for the dogs and cats. Finally he was ready to get into his truck. His intention was to see Winnie safely home, then go straight back to Silver Creek.

But when they arrived at Coffee Creek, it seemed only polite to offer to carry Bobby up the stairs for Winnie. Then he made a second trip with the Christmas tree, setting it in a bucket of water for Winnie to deal with later.

And then she invited him in—just for a few minutes. That was all it took for Winnie to change her sleeping little boy and have him settled in his crib in the new bedroom.

And then the two of them were alone.

A rare luxury.

He only meant to kiss her goodnight. But she responded so passionately that he had second thoughts.

He touched a strand of her hair, running it between his thumb and index finger, enjoying the silky softness. "I guess I should be a gentleman and leave."

Winnie tilted her head and gave him a provocative sideways look. "Or maybe you should be a gentleman and stay."

He swallowed, then cupped her head in his hand, holding her still so she had to look at him. "If I stay, I won't be a gentleman."

WINNIE HAD NEVER SEEN Jackson's eyes this dark. They were almost black. He seemed fascinated by her face. One second her mouth. The next her eyes. Then her mouth again. He traced his finger over her bottom lip.

"You want me to stay, Win?"

She was almost trembling from how much she desired him. He'd worn a charcoal sweater today and she dared to slip her hands under it, to feel the cords of muscles running across his back.

He sucked in a breath, then did the same to her, gliding his hands under her sweater, then up from her waist to her ribcage. Slowly he moved his hands higher, flicked open her bra then pulled her in tight.

"Kiss me," he demanded, his voice husky.

And when she did, something released in him. It was like a power surge. And suddenly he was out of control, kissing her, holding down her wrists and moving his lips down her neck, inch by sensuous inch.

She had guessed he was holding back the other times they'd been alone together. She'd been right.

"Oh, Jackson."

He pulled back, eyes hooded, voice deep and rough. "Should I stop?"

"Never."

MORNING CAME much too early. Jackson had stayed the night, and though they'd only slept for a few hours of it, Winnie couldn't remember the last time she'd went down so deeply.

"Morning, beautiful." Jackson's scruffy morning beard scraped her chin as he gave her a tender kiss.

She put a hand on the side of his face, holding him close for a while longer. "You are…amazing."

He laughed, but seemed a little embarrassed, too.

"You're not used to staying the night, are you?"

"Not my specialty," he agreed. "Until now."

The look he gave her held so much love, she felt a happiness so complete it was almost awe. To think that this gorgeous, strong male should want to be hers.

And then reality struck, reminding her she was, above all, a mother.

"Up, Mama. Up, up, up!"

She groaned and pulled herself to her elbows. "Mama's coming, Bobby."

"Let me get him," Jackson offered. A second later he was out of bed, slipping on his jeans and pulling the sweater over his head on his way out the door.

Winnie relaxed back into the pillow and closed her eyes. One more minute, then she'd get up…

The apartment was small. The walls thin. She heard Jackson. "Hey there, Bobby. Are you hungry?"

And then Bobby squealed, "Dada! Up, Dada, up!"

Winnie's hand flew to her throat. She jumped from the bed in one quick flowing movement, grabbing her housecoat from the back of a chair. A second later Jackson was at the entrance to her room.

"Bobby needs you," he said.

Everything was different. His eyes, his expression, his body language. He was like another man. Very distant and unapproachable.

"I have to go," he said.

And then he did.

WHAT HAD HE DONE? Oh, God, what had he done?

Jackson took the stairs two at a time, not bothering to put on the jacket he'd grabbed on his way out the door until he reached the truck he'd left parked outside the Cinnamon Stick last night.

The town was quiet this early on Monday morning. But his head was full of sounds. A little boy, *Brock's* little boy, calling him Dada.

The sound of it had broken his heart.

I'm not your daddy. Your daddy is dead. You'll never even meet him. And it's because of me....

He'd thought he was over the guilt, ready to move forward, but he'd been wrong.

He started the truck's engine, then brushed four inches of snow from the windshield. The day was cold, but the sky was clear.

The storm was over.

But inside his heart, it had just begun.

WINNIE DIDN'T HEAR a word from Jackson all that day. Or the next. She hardly slept either night and didn't have much of an appetite, either. She had to do something to get rid of these knots in her stomach, and calling Jackson didn't seem like the smart thing.

Finally she was so desperate, she actually went back into the kitchen to talk to Vince.

He was sprinkling yeast over a glass bowl filled with warm milk. "Shut that door."

She guessed he meant for her to be on the other side of it, but she did as he asked.

"I need your advice, Vince." She perched on a stool, resting her feet on one of the rungs and leaning back against the counter.

"You've come to the wrong place for that."

It was true, not many people would think about approaching the gruff, ex-bronc rider for his thoughts on matters of the heart. But in this case, Winnie figured he was the perfect choice.

"Things were going so well between Jackson and me. And then Bobby called him daddy. And it spooked him. He went running and hasn't talked to me in two days."

"Daddy, huh?"

"Well, *dada* to be exact. I'm not sure Bobby even knows what it means, though maybe he does. Every time she sees him, Olive shows him pictures of Brock and says *daddy* about a thousand times. Or maybe he picked it up from the time he's spent with Laurel, Corb and Stephanie."

Vince rubbed a hand along the side of his unshaven cheek. "Is Jackson kind of uncomfortable around your kid?"

"No. He's great with Bobby. He's a natural dad."

"So it's not the role of caring for a child that frightens him."

"Not at all. It's the fact that this child belongs to Brock. Jackson feels guilty that he's taking over Brock's life. Especially since he was the one driving when Brock died."

Vince rubbed his chin. "I figured he moved to Silver Creek Ranch to put some distance between himself and the Lamberts. But he'll never really be free of them. Not if you two stay together. Because Bobby is a Lambert and always will be."

Winnie pressed a hand to her forehead. "It's such a mess, isn't it? I felt guilty, too, in the beginning. But I'd grieved for Brock for a year and a half and I realized I was ready to move on. Why can't Jackson?"

"We don't all heal at the same rate. And Jackson, he's had a difficult life. His mother had troubles, with drugs and such. And even once he went to live on Coffee Creek Ranch, he had his trials. Olive didn't want him there. And he knew it."

"I realize he had a rough childhood. But why does that make it so hard for him to love me?"

"It's not loving you that's hard. It's giving himself permission to be happy."

Vince's words rang true. Winnie looked at her baker with respect. "That's it. How the heck did a bachelor like you get to be so wise?"

"Aw, heck." Vince waved his hand as if he were shooing away a fly. "I'm no Dear Abby."

Despite her worries, Winnie had to laugh, imagining a picture of the wiry old cowboy above a Dear Abby column.

"Your advice is probably just as good as hers."

"Who'd want to listen to an old man who's made as many mistakes as I have?"

She supposed he was talking about his drinking problem. "At least the only person you harmed was yourself."

"I wish that was true."

"What do you mean?"

"Never you mind. Just get the hell out of here. And don't let in a draft or the yeast won't rise."

IF THIS WASN'T REAL, then why could he feel the sun on his face? The roof of the SUV was gone and the airbag had Jackson pressed tightly against the back of his seat.

The three of them had been singing along with the radio, a rowdy song about getting knocked down and getting up again.

But the music was off now, like the engine. Outside Jackson could hear some robins calling back and forth. They sounded worried.

He shouldn't look. He knew it would be awful. But he couldn't stop himself. Slowly he turned his head to the passenger side of the vehicle.

Brock. Oh, God. No. So much blood.

He closed his eyes. Swallowed. Then called to the backseat. "Corb? You okay?"

No answer.

He must have killed them both.

"No!" Jackson shot up from his pillow.

He was in bed. It was still dark.

Hell. The nightmares were back. With a vengeance.

He waited a minute for his heart to stop thundering, then made his way to the washroom, where he rinsed the slick coating of sweat from his face.

He checked the time on his phone. Five-thirty. He might as well do the chores. Downstairs, as he put on his warmest clothes, the dogs sleeping in Maddie's room heard him and came to follow him outdoors.

He almost welcomed the bitter cold. This was the third night he'd woken this way. Jackson was living in his own personal hell again, and he knew he deserved it.

He must have been crazy to think he could take Brock's place in Winnie's life and not pay the consequences.

Olive had been right, after all. That was one of the most annoying things about her. She often was.

After a quick romp in the snow, Trix and Honey went into the barn while he loaded bales on Maddie's old flatbed truck. When he had enough hay, he drove out to the feed bunk, following the trail he'd cleared through the snow after the last storm. The cows were huddled together under the shelter. Kind of a pathetic herd now, but in a few years, that would change.

Snow and even a few icicles clung to the cattle's dark coats. He tossed their bales into the feed bunk, then checked to make sure the heaters were working and the water wasn't frozen.

He drove back to the barn, where he fed the horses and mucked out their stalls. It was warmer in here, but not toasty. He thought longingly of the Lamberts' heated, high-tech barns. It would be at least a decade before he'd have anything that fancy here at Silver Creek.

He was about to head into the house, anticipating that first cup of hot coffee, when he heard the barn door open.

He turned to see the baker from the Cinnamon Stick, Vince Butterfield. He had on a heavy sheepskin jacket, but still the old cowboy looked cold.

"Hell of a morning."

"Welcome to Montana in December." He couldn't imagine what Vince was doing here, and a terrible thought occurred to him. "Are Win and her son okay?"

Vince held up a reassuring hand. "They're fine." He let out a long breath. "Look, I know you must be surprised to see me. But can we talk for a bit?"

"Don't see why not. I'm finished here. Let's go inside and I'll make some coffee."

"If it's okay with you, I'd rather talk in my vehicle. It's nice and warm."

Jackson looked the older man in the eyes. It was a strange request. But he supposed it had to do with the history between Vince and Maddie. "Maddie'll still be in bed, if that's what's worrying you."

"I don't want to run the risk of disturbing her."

Vince seemed uncomfortable. Maybe even nervous. "Fine."

Jackson made sure to close the barn door behind them. Parked beside his own truck was Winnie's little SUV with the decal of the steaming latte on the back window.

The surprise of seeing her vehicle made him freeze for a moment.

"She doesn't know I borrowed her car. I shouldn't really be driving at all since I don't have a license."

Jackson remembered then that Vince's only mode of transportation was a bicycle, even though he'd been sober for several years now.

As he walked alongside the other man toward the idling vehicle, Jackson noticed their strides were exactly the same length.

They parted at the SUV, each heading to a different door. Once inside, Jackson looked at the older man again. "So what's this about?"

"Winnie came to talk to me yesterday. She's very upset."

"Oh, hell." Why would Winnie talk to this old coot about their personal problems?

"I'm not a fan of butting my nose into other people's problems." Vince grasped the steering wheel with both hands, facing out the front window instead of looking at Jackson. "But don't you think that little lady has been through enough?"

Jackson felt sick to his stomach at the thought of Winnie hurting. Because of him.

"It was a mistake to get involved in the first place. I wish I could undo it. And I wish I hadn't hurt her. But it's too late now."

"Too late because you don't love her?"

Right. As if it was even possible for him to *not* love her.

"I do love her. But it's wrong. I'm the last person who should be trying to take Brock's place in her life. He was practically my brother." Jackson's voice choked in his throat.

He swallowed. Forced himself to say the rest. "Bobby called me his daddy the other day. *Me.* When it should have been—" His voice failed him again, and he stared out the side window bleakly. The dogs were sitting at the door to the house, waiting for him to let them inside. "I've got to go."

As he groped for the door handle, Vince grasped his arm. The old guy had a real tough grip.

"We're not finished. The dogs will be okay for five more minutes."

"I have nothing more to say."

"Really? Well, I was hoping you could explain something to me. If you love Winnie, why is Bobby seeing you as a father figure such a deal breaker?"

"Isn't it obvious?"

"You feel guilty about his father dying. Well, how does that help Bobby?" When Jackson didn't answer, Vince tried a different tack. "You grew up without a dad, didn't you? How was that?"

Hell. Jackson gave the old guy a dirty look. "What would you know about me and my childhood?"

"More than you would guess."

A sudden cold rippled down Jackson's spine. It had nothing to do with the weather. And everything to do with the man sitting beside him. "What are you trying to tell me?"

Chapter Fourteen

"I hate talking about my past. It's nothing to be proud of." Vince was hanging on to the wheel again, as if he could steer his way out of this conversation.

Jackson had a feeling he wouldn't like what was coming, either. But he felt as pinned to his seat as if the air bag had exploded and was holding him there.

"I grew up in Coffee Creek, but I left town when I was twenty. I wanted to be a rodeo cowboy. And I got what I wanted. I spent most of my adult life following the circuit, and most of that time I was also an alcoholic."

Jackson knew all this. But hearing the pain in Vince's voice as he recounted the story of his past made it seem all the more real. And sad.

"Maddie Turner and I were high school sweethearts. I wanted her to marry me and live my vagabond lifestyle. She turned me down. Can't blame her. I didn't offer her much. Over the years I turned to different women. One of them was a pretty gal who liked to drink almost as much as I did." He hesitated, then added, "Your mother."

In the silence that followed, Jackson wondered if he'd heard right. "You can't be saying..."

"I'm your father."

Jackson shifted in his seat and stared at him. Searching the face that he'd never paid much attention to before, he suddenly noticed similarities. The line of his jaw. The color of his eyes. Before Vince had gone gray, his hair had probably been almost black, like Jackson's.

"I was drinking heavily in those days. I went to Maddie for advice. We were still friends and I saw her every time I passed through town. She told me I should sober up and marry your mother. But I couldn't. So I gave your mother the sum total of my savings, which was about thirty thousand dollars, and that was it. I never saw her again."

Jackson didn't know what to think. Or how to feel. He'd gone kind of numb, he figured. "Why didn't you tell me this sooner?"

"What's the point? It's sure as hell too late for me to be any sort of real father. The only reason I'm telling you now is so you'll think about Bobby and what's best for him. Do you think the memory of a dead father will be enough? Was having an absent father enough for you?"

Vince knew the answer, of course.

Just as Jackson did.

Bob Lambert had been the answer to his deepest prayers. But Bob hadn't made an appearance in Jackson's life until he was thirteen years old. He would have given *anything* to have had a dad like Bob from the start.

"You're comparing Bobby to me—it's not the same thing. His dad died. You just opted out of my life."

"That's true," Vince agreed. "But I grew up without

a father, too. And I'm not sure the *reason* a boy doesn't have a father matters. You feel the void all the same."

JACKSON GOT OUT of Winnie's car, feeling like a different man than the one he'd been ten minutes ago. He didn't turn and look as Vince drove off. It was going to take some time to adjust to the fact that the old cowboy was his biological father.

Right now he just felt numb about the whole thing.

The dogs came running toward him eagerly. They were anxious to get inside.

He didn't seem to care about anything, himself. He went through his usual routine in a fog. Giving the dogs their breakfast, putting on coffee and preparing Maddie's cereal.

He heard her coughing as he approached her room, but by the time he knocked, the fit had ended.

"Come in," she said, her voice weak and tremulous.

"Good morning, Maddie." She looked more pale than usual. He set down the tray, then opened the drapes. "Are you okay?" When he turned around, Maddie had raised her eyebrows.

"I should be asking that about you. Are you all right, Jackson?"

Hell, no, was the right answer. But, of course, he wouldn't say that.

"You're the patient, not me. How was your night?"

She sighed. "Not bad." She dipped her spoon in the cereal, hesitated then placed the small amount of food in her mouth.

Vince Butterfield was his father, Jackson thought, as he went back to clean up the kitchen.

Vince Butterfield is my dad.

He didn't know when it would sink in. If it would ever feel real.

But what did feel all too real was knowing he'd hurt Winnie. Vince had been right about that—she didn't deserve it. The fact that he was hurting too—because God, how he missed her—that didn't matter. He'd broken his rule, gotten involved, slept with her and created expectations...

Then bolted.

It was wrong, he saw now, to have put his guilt ahead of Winnie's happiness and security.

One more thing Vince was right about. He could be a good father to Bobby. He felt it in his bones. Just the way he'd known, when he'd first landed on Coffee Creek Ranch, that he'd found the sort of life where he belonged.

Jackson spent the morning doing chores around the house, then making Maddie some soup for lunch. She was settled in her easy chair in the sitting room now, and after he'd made sure she was comfortable, he asked if she'd be okay if he went into town for an hour or two.

"Of course." She gave him a concerned look, but said nothing further.

He drove straight to the Cinnamon Stick. It was one-thirty. He was glad to see that no vehicles were parked by the café. The lunch rush must be over.

He hesitated before stepping inside. For a long time he'd avoided this café, the way he'd avoided Winnie. Knowing she belonged to another man, and knowing how much he wanted her, he hadn't really had a choice.

But so much had changed.

And now he was here to see if Winnie would give him another chance.

QUIET MOMENTS WERE bad for the bottom line. But right now, Winnie was thankful they had no customers. She turned on the dishwasher, then went to wipe down the tables, only to discover Dawn had already taken care of it.

"Why don't you take a quick break for lunch now?" Winnie suggested.

"Thanks. Mind if I dash over to the post office? I ordered the cutest pair of shoes online and I want to see if they've arrived yet."

Winnie laughed. "Sure. Go ahead." Dawn was lucky she still lived at home or she'd never be able to afford her shopping habit.

The young blonde slipped on the coat she'd bought only a month ago, then skipped out the door. Finding herself alone, Winnie sank onto a stool and allowed her head to sink onto the counter.

The past three days had been *miserable*. Hardest of all had been putting on a brave face to friends, employees and customers. It was different when Brock had died. Back then everyone had understood that she was falling apart. They'd been supportive and kind.

But now her heart had been broken and nobody knew. She hadn't even admitted to Laurel how badly she felt. Mostly because she doubted her friend would understand. For some reason Laurel just couldn't see that Jackson was *it* for her.

The doorbell chimed and a gust of cool air snaked across her back. Winnie jolted upright and put on a smile, then turned around to face her new customer.

But it was Jackson in the doorway. He'd shut the door but was rooted to the welcome mat.

Her heart skipped and jumped at the sight of him.

Traitorous heart.

She felt her smile slip away until her lips were drawn in a hard, thin line.

"What are you doing here?" She crossed her arms over her chest, backing up toward the kitchen.

Jackson never came to her café. So why now?

She thought back to that morning, seeing Vince park her car in the usual spot before slipping the keys back on the hook and going back to the kitchen.

She'd wondered what he'd been up to.

And now she knew. He'd gone to talk to Jackson. Probably told him he'd better do right by Winnie Hays, or else.

It had been sweet of Vince to try.

But totally misguided.

"Think I could get a coffee? One of those cinnamon buns, too?"

Did he really think it would be that easy? "I'm taking a break right now."

He nodded. "Okay. Well, the real reason I came was to apologize."

He looked miserable. Which made her angry. He was the one who had run out, who'd trampled all over her heart and her feelings.

And *he* was miserable?

"Sometimes apologies aren't enough."

"You're right. But they still have to be said." He moved across the room, stopping at the counter then laying his hands flat on the surface that stood between them. "I panicked that night. I acted like an idiot and a fool. Especially considering I'd just spent the night with the woman of my dreams."

His words nestled into her heart, finding a soft spot

she hadn't yet protected. She took a deep breath. *Don't be a fool, Winnie. Don't fall for this again.*

"Let me guess. You felt guilty when Bobby called you daddy."

"Of course I did."

She shook her head. There was no *of course* about it. But he didn't see that. She didn't think he ever would.

"I'm sorry I hurt you that night. I acted like a jerk. Can you forgive me, Win? Give me another chance?"

She had to look away from him then. Because there was still something about his eyes that drew her in. She had a feeling it would always be this way between them. Which only made this more painful, knowing they could have had something so powerful and good.

"What are you asking for, Jackson? Another chance to feel guilty because you're alive and Brock isn't?"

His brow furrowed as he took in her words. "I'll always feel bad about that. But that doesn't mean I can't love you. And Bobby, too."

"Actually, it does. As long as you keep hanging on to that guilt of yours, nothing is going to change."

"You're acting as if I have a choice about how I feel," he said bitterly. "But if I could turn my emotions on and off so easily, I would have talked myself out of loving you long ago."

"Well, maybe you should keep working on it."

He went silent, then said softly, "You can't mean that."

"You've given me no choice. Now, please leave, Jackson. I'd like to make room for the *real* customers."

JACKSON SPED BACK to Silver Creek faster than was safe, but damn it, he'd pretty much had enough. He'd apologized, hadn't he? Why was Winnie being so bullheaded about this?

But by the time he'd pulled up to the ranch house, he'd calmed down enough to acknowledge the truth in what she'd said. As long as he felt guilty about Brock, he'd never be able to love Winnie the way she deserved. And he couldn't be the father that Bobby needed, either.

They were both, in the long run, going to be better off without him.

The same would not hold true for him.

Winnie had been his sunshine, his joy. He'd never replace her in his life. And no amount of time would change that.

He grabbed the bags of groceries he'd picked up in town and made his way to the kitchen. "Maddie, I'm back. Everything okay?"

"Fine, thank you." Maddie's voice traveled faintly from the sitting room.

"Would you like some tea?"

"That would be lovely."

He filled the kettle and placed it on the hot cast-iron stove, then put away the groceries. Five minutes later, he carried a tray to the sitting room.

Maddie seemed to be shrinking a little more every day. His heart constricted when he saw how small and helpless she looked as she smiled at him.

"You're a blessing, Jackson."

"I'm glad someone thinks so."

Her eyes settled on him with keen interest. "Are you finally ready to tell me what's been going on with you these past few days?"

"It's complicated."

"I have time to listen."

She sounded so calm and unjudgmental that he could feel the bands around his chest loosen. He perched on the stool by her chair and stroked one of the dogs at her feet. Honey or Trix. He still couldn't tell them apart.

"Winnie and I have been having problems. It's my fault. I kind of freaked out when I realized her son was seeing me as a father figure."

"Why would that frighten you? You seem to love his mother. And you're so good at looking after people and animals who need you."

Was he? He was kind of honored that she would describe him that way. "It's because I feel guilty about stepping in on Brock's turf. People keep telling me to get over it, but I can't. And then Vince showed up this morning and—"

"Wait a minute. Vince Butterfield was here?" Maddie pressed a hand to her chest.

"Yup. Came into the barn when I was doing chores. He was mad at me for hurting Winnie. And he told me the most incredible story." Jackson swallowed, wondering if he could say the words out loud. Maybe it would help make it feel less surreal. "About being my father."

"Finally. I was wondering if he would ever do it."

Jackson wondered if this woman would ever stop surprising him. "You've known all along?"

"I, too, have played a larger role in your life than you realize, Jackson. But I couldn't tell you until Vince was ready to reveal the fact that he was your biological father."

Jackson stared into the face that he thought he knew so well. "Is this where you finally explain why you're planning to leave me your ranch?"

She smiled. "It's funny in a way. You and I have

one thing in common—we've both lived with guilt for a very long time. The difference is that yours is self-inflicted. You had no way of avoiding that moose. But me, I hurt Vince badly when I refused to marry him."

"But if you didn't love him, you didn't have a choice, either."

"Oh, I did love him. But I couldn't leave my father. He had no one by then. He'd never gotten over losing our mother, and I was all he had left. So I said no to Vince's proposal and stayed on at Silver Creek. I wish I could say I never regretted that decision, but it wouldn't be true."

It was ironic, Jackson thought, how the two sisters had both paid a price for the love of their father. Olive had suffered because she had too little. And Maddie had suffered because she had too much.

"Vince didn't take my refusal well," Maddie continued. "He started drinking. And taking up with casual affairs. He'd never been like that before. And then he got your mother pregnant, and though I begged him to do the honorable thing, he was too far gone with his drinking."

"He told me all of that."

"Good. But I bet he didn't tell you that when your mother got into trouble with the law and you were put into the foster program, he came to me and pleaded with me to look after you."

"He did?" Suddenly it was impossible to sit still. Jackson got up and paced to the window. Shoving a hand through his hair, he asked, "What did you do?"

"I couldn't see taking in a thirteen-year-old boy on my own. So I asked Bob Lambert to do it."

"I didn't think Bob and you were on speaking terms in those days."

"Not officially. Bob wanted to support his wife. He really did love Olive, you know. But he had a good heart, and he worried about me living out here on my own. Just the way his youngest son would do when he was older, Bob looked in on me now and then. And he agreed to go see you and think about taking you to live on Coffee Creek Ranch."

"That was the best thing you could have done for me."

"I'm glad it worked out well. But I know Olive has never really accepted you into the family. That's why I wanted to give you Silver Creek."

Jackson looked at her worn, frail face with wonder. She'd done so much for him. But was it too much?

"I don't need to own a ranch. I could always find work as a foreman or hired hand."

"You could. But I have this selfish desire to have Silver Creek Ranch become a vibrant, successful cattle ranch again. If I left the ranch to one of Olive's children, the operation would be merged in with Coffee Creek. But you, Jackson, you could bring this place back to life."

"It means that much to you?"

"Oh, yes. I didn't have children of my own, so this ranch is my legacy. And in a strange and twisted way, you are the closest thing I ever had to a son."

Chapter Fifteen

Jackson took a week to absorb the startling news about his father's identity and Maddie's subsequent role in his life. He wished he could talk to Winnie about it all, but she'd replied to his attempts to text her with a request that he give her some space.

So he turned to Corb, who, now that Brock was gone, was the closest friend he had. They went out for a few beers at the Lonesome Spur in town and Corb was astounded to hear that Vince Butterfield was Jackson's father and that Maddie had been behind Bob Lambert's decision to take him in as a foster son.

"Holy crap." Corb pushed both his hands through his thick blond hair. "Vince, your dad? I never would have guessed.... Though now that I think of it, you're the same height and similar builds."

"Still, it's crazy, right?"

"And Maddie actually asked my dad to take you in. That's another tough thing to believe. All of us kids have memories of our dad walking right by her in town without so much as a nod of recognition."

"I guess he was torn between his own sense of what was right, and being loyal to your mother. Maddie says he used to check on her once in a while. And when her border collie was expecting, he asked if she would give one of the pups to Cassidy."

"I'll tell my sister that. She's never known the whole story before. When she found Sky in a basket on the front porch on her birthday, Dad couldn't stop smiling—so we figured he was behind the gift. Mom pretended to be pleased, but we could tell she was furious. She would have known the pup came from Silver Creek. But I wonder if she also guessed then that Dad sometimes talked to Maddie."

They'd finished their first beer by then. Corb nodded at the server to bring them another. Then he folded his arms on the table and leaned in closer.

"So. What's going on with you and Winnie? Laurel says she's never seen her friend this miserable. Given what she's been through the past few years, that's saying something."

Jackson closed his eyes briefly. He hated hearing that she was suffering. Again. And it was his fault. Again.

"I should have listened to what everyone was saying and kept my distance."

"You really think that's true?"

"Don't you?"

"At first, I did," Corb admitted. "And so did Laurel. But then I got to thinking what I would have wanted if *I'd* been the one to die in that car crash."

It had almost happened, Jackson reflected, thinking of Corb's coma and long recovery.

"If Laurel had been left on her own—she was pregnant, too, at the time, though she didn't yet know it. What would I want for her?"

"And?"

"I'd want her to be with a guy who loved her. I'd want Stephanie to have a dad to protect her."

"Really? You could be that generous?"

Corb sat back in his chair and met Jackson's gaze straight on. "What kind of man would I be if I wasn't?"

CORB'S WORDS LINGERED in Jackson's mind all night long. He didn't sleep much, but when he awoke he felt oddly invigorated.

That morning, after chores, he asked Maddie if she would mind if he did a few renovations around the place. December was a notoriously slow month on a ranch and he had too much time on his hands.

"This place could sure use a face-lift," Maddie agreed. She looked curious, but didn't ask him for any more explanation. She knew when to talk and when to be silent.

Affection for the older woman welling up in his heart, Jackson stooped to give her a hug, then headed to the hardware store to buy some supplies.

He resisted the urge to stop in to see Winnie. He knew he needed time to let his conversation with Corb really sink in.

Besides, this time he had to do it right.

He had a plan.

And only two and a half weeks to execute it.

"EIGHTEEN DAYS UNTIL Christmas," Winnie sighed. "I've decorated our tree and baked a batch of shortbread, and that's it. I haven't even started my shopping."

Laurel had stopped in at the Cinnamon Stick after buying groceries for the week and Winnie was glad to see her. It had been a long day.

Make that a long week.

A couple of times a day Jackson had sent her text messages saying he needed to talk to her. She'd turned him down the first time and simply ignored the subsequent requests. She wasn't intending to be mean, she simply didn't think her heart could withstand seeing him again. She knew she had to stay the course. A clean break would be easier in the long run.

And yet a part of her wondered what he'd wanted to say.

She'd never know now, though. It had been more than a day since his last text.

And while she ought to be relieved that he'd finally taken the hint, of course she wasn't. She felt sadder than ever.

"I finished my list last weekend," Laurel admitted.

"You always were the organized one."

"Let me take Bobby tomorrow afternoon and you can go shopping in Lewistown," Laurel offered.

"Really?"

"Sure. It's always fun to let the rug rats play together." Though Bobby and Stephanie didn't really play with each other yet, they did seem to get a kick out of being together.

"That would be awesome. I really need to get my parents' gifts in the mail soon or they won't make it to Arizona in time."

She'd buy a few gifts for Bobby, as well. Not too many, because she had a strong suspicion his grandparents—especially Olive—would be spoiling him rotten.

She also wanted to buy something for Laurel and for Stephanie. And gifts for her staff. And she mustn't forget Olive.

"My pleasure. Corb and I wanted a quiet day at home anyway. And speaking of my darling husband, I have news."

"Oh?"

"Last night he went out to the bar with Jackson."

Winnie pulled back. "I'm not sure I want to hear this."

"I think you should." Laurel leaned forward and lowered her voice. "Vince went to visit Silver Creek a few days ago...."

Winnie nodded. She'd figured as much.

"He and Jackson had a private chat, and Vince confessed that he'd once had an affair with Jackson's mother."

Winnie frowned. She'd noticed her baker had been even more testy than usual the past few days, so she hadn't called him out for interfering. But this was not at all what she'd been thinking was behind the covert trip.

"Are you saying that Vince is Jackson's father?"

"Yes."

"Good Lord." Winnie sank onto a stool and tried to process this.

"Think about it," Laurel said. "They're almost exactly the same height and build. They both have blue eyes, and I'll bet Vince's hair was dark, too, before it turned gray."

Not only that, Winnie thought, but there was something about their smiles. Maybe she would have picked up on the similarity earlier if Vince's teeth weren't so brown from years of smoking and poor care.

"Quite the shocking bit of news, huh?"

Winnie nodded.

"But there's more. Maddie finally told Jackson the

entire story of her romance with Vince. It turns out that he *did* ask her to marry him, but she couldn't leave her dad alone on the ranch, so she said no."

"Did Maddie love him?"

"Yes. But she felt obliged to her father."

"Oh, poor Maddie. And poor Vince… Do you think that's why he started drinking?"

"Maddie said it was. And there's more…"

Laurel went on to explain how it was that Bob Lambert came to be Jackson's foster father. Maddie had been behind it all. Winnie's head was spinning by the time Laurel finally left to go back to Coffee Creek Ranch.

So many things that had seemed strange or coincidental suddenly made sense. As did Jackson's flurry of text messages. He must have been trying to tell her about all of this.

And not, as she'd secretly hoped, been hoping to woo her back to him.

THE NEXT DAY, Corb dropped into town to pick up Bobby, as Laurel had promised.

"How's it going, Winnie?"

"Fine."

"Really?" Corb raised his eyebrows pointedly.

She supposed he was referring to her appearance, which she knew wasn't great. The sleepless nights were catching up to her.

"I really appreciate you and Laurel taking Bobby for the day."

"Hey, we're his aunt and uncle. Anytime you need a break, we're happy to help."

Gosh, but Laurel had been lucky, marrying a great

guy like Corb. Easygoing and uncomplicated—the exact opposite of Jackson.

And yet, underneath the layers of complex emotions, Jackson was a good man, too. She could admit it. Even if she was mad as hell at him right now.

She bundled Bobby into his snowsuit and boots, then walked out to the truck with Corb, tucking the diaper bag into the space below Bobby's feet.

"Bye-bye, baby boy." She kissed his forehead. "Have fun with Auntie Laurel and Stephanie."

"Fee!" He started kicking his boots against his seat, his standard move when he was excited. "Fee, Fee, Fee!"

Corb gave her a quizzical look.

"His name for your daughter," she explained.

"Ah." Corb grinned, then touched the brim of his hat in farewell.

Winnie stepped back to the sidewalk and watched them drive off. Then she grabbed her purse and shopping list and headed to Lewistown.

She felt melancholic as she strolled down the main shopping street. It seemed that most of the shoppers today were couples, strolling arm in arm along the snow-covered sidewalks, pointing out items in the decorated shop windows, whispering hints about what they'd really like for Christmas.

Winnie stuck to her list, and within two hours she had everything she needed, but felt no sense of satisfaction about it.

Where was the joy of Christmas when your heart was broken?

She'd been so foolish to take the risk of getting involved with Jackson. And yet, looking back on the six weeks since her return to Coffee Creek, she couldn't decide what she would have done differently. Because if she hadn't at least given a relationship with Jackson a try, she would have always wondered what if.

But was it any better being left with if only?

CHRISTMAS WAS A major occasion on Coffee Creek Ranch. Jackson knew this well, having lived there for over seventeen years. Olive spared no expense with the decorations. He'd helped Corb and B.J. bring in a tree that had to be at least fourteen feet tall and then watched as Olive, Savannah and Laurel loaded it with ornaments, garlands and lights that would do the tree in Rockefeller Center proud.

That had been a week ago.

And now here was B.J., knocking on the back door at Silver Creek then stepping into the kitchen where Jackson was stirring a can of paint, getting ready to put the final touch on his renovation projects.

"Oh, boy," B.J. said when he saw the painting supplies laid out on the floor. "I hope you don't need help with that. Savannah wants me home this afternoon to welcome Regan back from her first term at med school."

"Nah. I can handle it." He waited for the eldest Lambert son to get to the point. It didn't take long.

"Mom was wondering if you're coming to Christmas Eve dinner tomorrow night. And she wants you to bring Maddie. Will she come, do you think?"

"Of course I will," Maddie replied from the other room.

B.J. grinned. "Well, there's my answer. We're having drinks at five, dinner at six. See you then!"

And he was off, before Jackson could find a way of

discreetly inquiring if Winnie would be there. But surely she would. Olive would want her grandson present.

The big surprise was that she had invited her older sister.

He went to the sitting room to see how Maddie felt about it. "So? What do you make of being invited to Coffee Creek Ranch?"

Maddie was reclined on her usual chair, with her cat Ginger sleeping on her lap. Slowly her translucent eyelids fluttered open. "I'm sure it was hard for Olive to do. But I'm grateful she did."

"Grateful? That's generous of you after all the years she treated you like an outcast."

"And why shouldn't I be generous? It's a good thing to be. Especially at this time of year, and at my stage of life."

"But isn't it hard? I mean, don't you feel any bitterness at all? Especially now—when you ended up with this stupid cancer. It isn't fair." It made him angry—really pissed—when he thought about it. Maddie was a sweet, kindhearted person who hadn't had many breaks in life.

Maddie smiled at him sadly. "It's such a common expression—*life isn't fair*—and yet people still seem blindsided when bad things happen to them or the people they care about."

"I guess you're right. It isn't logical to be mad. But that's how I feel. Did you even smoke?" He had never seen any sign that she did around the house or barns.

"No. But my father was a heavy smoker and they say secondhand smoke can be just as bad…." She shrugged. "At least I've had sixty-eight years. That's a lot more than my mother had."

There she was. Looking at the bright side again.

"You amaze me, Maddie."

"I'm not saying I don't have regrets. Because I do. But I'd feel better if I could believe that you might learn from some of my mistakes."

"Such as?" he asked cautiously, not sure he wanted to hear what she had to say.

"If I could boil it down to one sentence, it would be this. When it comes to love, you can never give too much."

She didn't add anything else, certainly didn't mention any names.

But he got the message, loud and clear.

And he could hardly wait to see Winnie at the family Christmas Eve dinner.

THE NEXT DAY Jackson could tell Maddie was excited about their upcoming visit to the Lamberts. She showered and fussed with her hair, and picked out a Christmas brooch to wear with her red sweater and gray pants.

The outfit was the gift he had given her, thanks to some online-shopping help from Laurel. The package had arrived from J. Crew in the mail last week. And the expression on Maddie's face when she'd opened it this morning had made all his efforts worthwhile.

She'd held the wool sweater to her cheek. "It's so pretty. And soft."

"I decided to give it to you early, so you could wear it to the party tonight. If you want."

"Oh, thank you, Jackson. I was wondering what on earth I was going to put on."

Because she'd lost so much weight, she swam in all her old clothes. And he was glad he'd managed to think of something that would make her smile. And feel good about herself.

He even took some time dressing himself, which wasn't usual for him. But he couldn't help wondering whether Winnie would prefer the dark gray shirt or the blue one.

He and Maddie arrived at Coffee Creek Ranch exactly at five. Winnie's car wasn't in the driveway yet. He assumed she'd be there shortly.

All the Lambert kids lined up to welcome their aunt into their home. Last was Olive. She hesitated, then gave her sister a tentative hug. "I'm glad you came."

"Well, thanks for inviting me."

The exchange was stiff and a little awkward, but it was a start, Jackson figured.

And then came the big surprise of the evening. Vince, who'd been hanging back in the family room, hidden on the other side of the Christmas tree, came out to say hello.

"Hope you don't mind me being here. Olive insisted." He shook Jackson's hand first, and Jackson gave him a short nod.

He was hoping, over time, that he and Vince would get to know one another better. But in his heart Bob Lambert would always be the man he thought of as a father.

Maddie was not so sanguine about the surprise visitor, however. "Oh, my," she whispered when she first spotted Vince. And then, when the old cowboy held out his hand, she sighed.

"I never thought I'd see you here."

"I wouldn't have come if you hadn't been invited. It's been too long, Maddie. Much too long." Vince helped

Maddie settle into a chair, leaving Jackson to head to the kitchen to pour her an eggnog. Laurel was by the fridge, too, filling Stephanie's sippy cup with fruit juice.

"So when do you think Win will get here?" he asked, not even trying to mask his anticipation.

"She isn't coming." Laurel gave him a sympathetic shrug. "She phoned half an hour ago to say Bobby is coming down with something."

He didn't know what to say at first. It hadn't even occurred to him that she might not be here. But the more he thought about it, the more he realized he should have expected this.

"Do you think there's really something wrong with Bobby?"

Laurel hesitated. "No. But she had to give some excuse, or Olive would have sent one of her sons to drag Winnie and Bobby over here."

And would that have been such a disaster? Yes. Because *he* was here. And Winnie would do anything, apparently, to avoid him. Including cutting herself and her son out of the family's Christmas celebrations.

"I wish you'd have told me this sooner. I would have stayed home."

Laurel looked miserable. "I'm sure Winnie wouldn't want you to do that. That's probably why she made the call last minute the way she did."

Right.

The evening seemed to go on forever after that. The only highlight was seeing how happy Maddie looked, even giving Vince a shy smile every now and then. No question that she was the guest of honor that evening. Someone was always sitting by her side, making sure she had everything she wanted and keeping her entertained with stories.

Even fourteen-year-old Sky, who'd come along with Farley and Cassidy for the evening, never left Maddie's side.

From most people's point of view, the evening went very well. Jackson figured he was the only one who didn't clear his plate and go back for seconds.

But he had no appetite tonight.

And was only waiting for the evening to end so he could come up with a plan B.

Because he wasn't letting Winnie go. Not without a battle.

An hour after dessert had been served and the Christmas gifts opened, Jackson started looking at his watch. He figured Maddie must be exhausted. But he hadn't realized how badly. When she tried to stand to leave, she fell back to the chair, overtaken by a bout of coughing which seemed to go on forever.

He grabbed her some water while Cassidy rubbed her back until finally the coughing subsided.

Farley, who was a large animal vet, not a doctor, ran out to his truck and came back with a stethoscope. He listened to her heart and checked her pulse. "I think she's fine. Just tired."

"You'll sleep here tonight," Olive decided.

"I don't want to be a bother. It's just a ten-minute drive."

"The cold air will start another coughing fit," Olive interjected. "So don't argue. The spare room is all made up and ready for you. If you're not feeling stronger in the morning, we'll drive you to the hospital in Great Falls."

For once no one seemed to mind Olive's bossy nature. Even Jackson had to agree that the plan was sound, especially when Cassidy and Farley decided to stay the night, too, in case anything went wrong.

"You sure you're okay?" Jackson checked with Maddie before leaving.

"I'll be fine." Her eyelashes fluttered as she struggled to keep her eyes open. "It's been a wonderful day. But I'm so tired. You'll…" Her voice trailed off then.

"I'll take care of things at home. Make sure the dogs and cats are fed."

She nodded. "Thank you," she said, her voice trailing off on the *you*.

Jackson kissed the top of her head, then went to say goodbye to the family. He could tell Olive was annoyed with him. No doubt she blamed him for the fact that her grandson hadn't been present tonight.

When he came to Vince, he just shook the older man's hand. Maybe there would come a day when he felt a connection to his biological father. But it was still too soon for that.

Chapter Sixteen

Christmas morning, Winnie's eyes were open the second she heard her son giving his usual morning greeting.

"Up, Mama! Up, up, up!"

Wearily, she rose and put on slippers and her housecoat.

Bobby didn't know it was Christmas, of course. Just as he didn't realize he'd missed out on the Lambert Christmas Eve celebrations last night.

If he'd been even one year older, she would have felt really guilty about depriving him of that.

But Bobby would be just as happy to open his gifts from his grandmother later today. She was going to call Olive in a few hours to tell her Bobby was miraculously better and could they drop in for a visit sometime this afternoon.

"Hey there, baby boy. Merry Christmas." She released Bobby from the captivity of his crib, changed his diaper and dressed him in flannel-lined overalls and a thick fleecy sweater.

He squirmed throughout the process, having spotted the stocking she'd helped him hang on the doorknob—since they had no fireplace—the previous evening.

Last night he didn't have a clue about the point behind what they were doing.

But he got it now.

"Toys!" he shouted, pointing at the stocking stuffed full with some picture books and socks and an inexpensive plastic truck.

"Just a minute, honey." She did up the last clasp on his overalls, then let him go. He ran on his stiff toddler legs to the stocking and soon he had everything pulled out and scattered on the floor.

Winnie took some pictures, then set down the camera and went to look out the window.

It had snowed. Again.

What a long winter this was going to be.

But it *was* pretty. A blanket of mist lay over the creek for which the town was named, and the trees on the banks were frosted with snow. Beyond the creek, the fields sparkled with new whiteness below a cornflower-blue sky.

A perfect day to take Bobby for a ride on his sled. She better get dressed and feed her son his breakfast.

But when it came time to make the oatmeal, she discovered her microwave wasn't working. Too tired to figure out what was wrong, she took Bobby down to the café, where she put on some coffee for herself, made Bobby his oatmeal and toasted some cinnamon buns.

She had a high chair for her customers, and she put Bobby in that, along with his sippy cup and some pieces of cinnamon bun for a treat. She spooned the oatmeal for her son, and was just about to pour herself a cup of coffee when a knock sounded on the front door.

What the heck? Who on earth expected the café to be open on Christmas morning?

Bobby's eyes brightened. He loved visitors.

Slowly Winnie went to the door and peered through the frosted glass.

She opened the door and there he was. The one person she couldn't admit she'd been hoping to see.

"Merry Christmas, Win."

He looked good. Too good. But she missed the smile in his eyes.

"Going to let me in?"

She was just stepping aside when Bobby caught sight of him.

"Dada!" He clapped his hands and repeated the word six times or so for good measure.

Winnie cringed. *Great timing, son.*

But Jackson didn't run this time. He plucked Bobby out of the high chair and up onto his broad shoulders. "Hey, buddy. Having a good Christmas?" He galloped around the café, as fast as a six-foot-tall man could gallop in such a confined space, and Bobby giggled—until he spotted his sippy cup and pointed to that.

Jackson returned her son to his chair and his partially eaten breakfast, then finally turned to her. "We need to talk."

She nodded. "Would you like some coffee first?"

"That sounds great."

"Okay." She poured two mugs full, then put out some more cinnamon buns. Jackson slid onto the stool next to hers and took a sip.

"God, you make good coffee, Win."

It had taken him long enough to figure that one out. She took a sip herself and fought back the urge to start talking. He had come here with something to say, and she was going to let him do it.

Jackson combed his dark hair with one hand. He studied the ceiling, then the floor, and finally he looked at her squarely.

She couldn't help feeling sorry for him. She knew putting his feelings into words wasn't easy for him.

But he had to do it.

"I'm sorry I hurt you when I ran off that morning. I thought I was over feeling guilty about Brock, but obviously I wasn't."

"So why are you here now?" She was afraid to get her hopes up. But it had to mean something, the way he'd gone to Bobby so easily, not seeming to mind this time that her son, for some reason, wanted to call him daddy.

"Corb and I had a good talk a while ago about Brock. He didn't say anything I hadn't heard before, but somehow the message got through this time. And it helped, it really did."

"I'm glad, Jackson." Whatever had happened between the two of them, she didn't want him living the rest of his life with a burden of guilt that he didn't deserve.

"Then yesterday, at Christmas Eve dinner—when you weren't there—I was pretty disappointed."

She glanced at her son, who had somehow worked the lid off his sippy cup and was now dunking the cinnamon bun bits into his juice. "I thought it would be easier—for both of us—if I stayed away."

"Did you know Olive invited Maddie? And Vince?"

She nodded. "Laurel told me."

"They didn't talk that much. But I saw the secret looks that passed between them when they thought the other one wouldn't notice. I think they really loved each other."

"That's sad."

"It's more than sad. It's tragic. And it got me thinking…" He moved closer, taking her hands and pulling her up so he could look more deeply into her eyes. "I don't want to be sixty years old, looking back on a life I spent alone, when I could have been with you."

"Jackson?" Was this really happening? Did she dare put her faith in the words he was saying?

"Which brings me to the main reason I'm here this morning."

"And that is…" She could feel the connection between them, like a physical bond. More than the contact of their hands and eyes, it was something of the spirit. Of the soul.

"Because I love you. Win, I loved you the first time I saw you. It wasn't right then, but it is right now. That is, if you—"

"I do, Jackson. I love you, too."

They moved together, kissing tenderly. Jackson stroked the back of her head, her cheek, then finished with a light kiss on her forehead. For Winnie the moment felt fragile, like a delicate layer of frost on the branch of a tree. The slightest breeze might spoil everything.

"I want to believe this is real."

"It is. Absolutely." Jackson took her hand and pressed it to his heart. "This is yours. All yours." He grinned. "And Bobby's, too, of course."

"You didn't seem to mind him calling you daddy this time."

"I was honored. I'm going to try to be to Bobby what Bob Lambert was to me."

Her doubts fell away then. She could feel in her heart that something had changed in Jackson. He'd grown more sure of himself, more solid. He would be the pillar she needed. The pillar she and Bobby *both* needed.

She kissed him again, telling him with her eyes and her actions how deeply he was loved and needed. And when she pulled back, he gave her an excited grin.

"I have a Christmas surprise. It's back at Silver Creek. Will you come with me?"

As if there was any doubt.

THE DOGS GREETED them at the door when Winnie and Jackson arrived thirty minutes later. It hadn't taken Winnie long to pack a bag for her son, tucking in a gift she hadn't been able to resist buying for Jackson.

Just in case, she'd thought at the time. Which only proved that sometimes it paid to be an optimist.

"So what's the big surprise?" She was glad for the warmth of the big stove as she pulled off Bobby's snowsuit and boots and then her own winter wear.

"Be patient," Jackson teased. "Would you like coffee? Tea?"

"Maybe later." On the drive over he'd explained that Maddie had been so worn out by the Christmas Eve festivities last evening that Olive had insisted she spend the night. "Should we call and see how Maddie is doing?"

But Jackson was already reaching for his phone and a few seconds later he was connected. "Hey, Cassidy, Merry Christmas."

The room was quiet enough that Winnie could hear

her answer. "Same to you, Jackson. You should come over. Farley and I are whipping up a marvelous brunch."

"Maybe later. I wanted to check on Maddie. Is she okay?"

"*Much* better this morning. She and Mom are sitting by the fireplace gabbing like two sisters who haven't seen each other in almost forty years."

Jackson grinned. "Which is what they are."

"Yeah. But it's pretty amazing to witness."

Winnie felt moisture gather in her eyes at the thought. The sisters' reconciliation was the best Christmas gift the Lambert family could have hoped for.

"I'm glad, Cass."

Winnie could tell by his voice that he was moved, too. He ended his call then and gave her a big hug.

She squeezed him back with all her might.

"Okay, now that we know Maddie's all right, it's time to show you your surprise." He scooped Bobby up on his shoulder, then took her by the hand.

"Where are we going?"

"I remember touring you around the barn, but we never made it to the house. You've seen the dining room and the sitting room," he said as he walked through each. Then he opened a door off a short hall. "This is Maddie's room."

Winnie took a short peek, then they went up a curving set of stairs. Four doors led off from a spacious landing.

"I've been doing some renovations lately. I was working on a list that you once gave me."

Her heart skipped. Was he serious? She held her breath as he opened the first door.

"This was once a spare bedroom."

The room was now painted a cheery yellow. There were empty shelving units on one wall. A pint-size sofa sat against another wall. And a tiny table and chair, made for kids, was in the center.

Bobby squirmed to be let down, and as soon as Jackson did so, he planted himself in the chair, looking terribly pleased with himself.

A playroom for Bobby...

She looked at Jackson, speechless with amazement.

Jackson fastened the child gate that had been installed at the top of the stairs, then took her hand and led her to the next room. It was empty, but freshly painted the same color as Bobby's room back at her apartment.

A good-size bedroom for Bobby...

She let her hand trail over the smooth walls. The room was at least double the size of the one they'd made in her apartment.

They went across the hall then, to the bathroom, where Jackson had also made some improvements. A new pedestal sink and, more importantly...*a big tub for soaking.*

There was a picture window across from the tub with a perfect view of Square Butte Mountain.

She squeezed his hand. "This is beautiful."

The next door led to the largest bedroom of all. "This is where I've been sleeping. But I converted an old sewing room into this. He opened two French doors and stepped back to let her see.

A walk-in closet.

"The house still needs a lot of work. As you can tell, the kitchen is original."

"I *love* that old kitchen. And I love you, too. You must have worked so hard to get all this done so fast."

"I was motivated."

She hugged him, then laughed. "It seems like you're trying to ask me something here."

"Going about it kind of ass-backward, aren't I? But will you marry me, Winnie Hays? Marry me and come to live on Silver Creek Ranch?"

"I will. And I promise you something. Together we're going to make this ranch into something special. We'll make Maddie Turner proud." She winked. "We may even give Coffee Creek Ranch a run for their money one day...."

Jackson whooped, circling his hands around her waist and twirling her in the air. Bobby came running then, curious and maybe a little frightened by all the ruckus. Jackson whisked him up and gave him the happy news.

"We're going to be a family, Bobby."

"Mine," Bobby said, matter-of-factly.

Could he possibly understand? No, he was much too young.

"When should we have the wedding?" She felt a little nervous just asking the question. The specter of the wedding-that-wasn't would loom heavily in her mind until she was officially Jackson's wife.

"If it's okay with you, I'd like it to happen quickly, so Maddie can be there."

"Yes. And let's make it small, just family."

He nodded. "Would December 31 be too fast?"

"As long as my parents can book some flights, I can't imagine a better way to bring in the new year."

THEY ENDED UP having the ceremony at Coffee Creek Ranch. Because the house was larger. Because the river rock fireplace would look great in the photos. And because Olive insisted.

"She never really changes, does she?" Winnie whispered to Jackson on the day they got together to plan the event.

"She's like a creek in the springtime. As long as you go with flow, it's all good."

Winnie laughed, because for the moment, going with the flow was fine with them both. All they wanted was to seal their commitment in front of family and friends. The menu and decor hardly mattered.

And yet Olive made it all perfect.

At seven o'clock on the evening of December 31, Winnie took a minute to think of Brock. Then she set aside that sadness and focused on her future.

With the help of Bonny and Eugenia, Olive had set up an elegant buffet in the dining room. The ceremony was to take place by the fireplace in candlelight. There were dozens of vanilla-scented pillar candles and glass bowls of pale pink roses.

"Ready, sweetheart?" Jackson, so handsome and fine in his one and only suit, held out his arm.

And she clung to it.

Together they walked down the hall toward the family room, entering it together.

And suddenly Winnie's nerves were gone, swept away by happiness as she saw the beloved faces of their family and friends.

Winnie's parents stood on one side of the enormous fireplace, along with Corb, Laurel, Stephanie and Bobby.

In the armchair was Maddie, with Vince planted on

one side and Farley, Cassidy and Sky seated at the floor by her feet.

Olive, dressed to the nines, as usual, was by the Christmas tree, which hadn't dared to dry out under her strict orders. She had her hand tucked into the arm of her eldest son. Savannah and her sister, Regan, were on B.J.'s other side.

Winnie smiled at all of them, then turned her gaze to the cowboy by her side.

The ceremony was short. Sweet. In ten minutes it was done. They were married.

In the distance, the coyotes howled. Maybe at the full moon. Maybe in approval.

Because if there was one thing Winnie had learned in the past eighteen months, it was that life was a precious gift. And she had every intention of making the most of hers and Jackson's and the family they would have together.

* * * * *

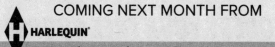

REQUEST YOUR FREE BOOKS!
2 FREE NOVELS PLUS 2 FREE GIFTS!

HARLEQUIN®

American ★ Romance®

LOVE, HOME & HAPPINESS

YES! Please send me 2 FREE Harlequin® American Romance® novels and my 2 FREE gifts (gifts are worth about $10). After receiving them, if I don't wish to receive any more books, I can return the shipping statement marked "cancel." If I don't cancel, I will receive 4 brand-new novels every month and be billed just $4.74 per book in the U.S. or $5.24 per book in Canada. That's a savings of at least 14% off the cover price! It's quite a bargain! Shipping and handling is just 50¢ per book in the U.S. and 75¢ per book in Canada.* I understand that accepting the 2 free books and gifts places me under no obligation to buy anything. I can always return a shipment and cancel at any time. Even if I never buy another book, the two free books and gifts are mine to keep forever.

154/354 HDN F4YN

Name _____ (PLEASE PRINT)

Address _____ Apt. #

City _____ State/Prov. _____ Zip/Postal Code

Signature (if under 18, a parent or guardian must sign)

Mail to the Harlequin® Reader Service:
IN U.S.A.: P.O. Box 1867, Buffalo, NY 14240-1867
IN CANADA: P.O. Box 609, Fort Erie, Ontario L2A 5X3

Want to try two free books from another line?
Call 1-800-873-8635 or visit www.ReaderService.com.

* Terms and prices subject to change without notice. Prices do not include applicable taxes. Sales tax applicable in N.Y. Canadian residents will be charged applicable taxes. Offer not valid in Quebec. This offer is limited to one order per household. Not valid for current subscribers to Harlequin American Romance books. All orders subject to credit approval. Credit or debit balances in a customer's account(s) may be offset by any other outstanding balance owed by or to the customer. Please allow 4 to 6 weeks for delivery. Offer available while quantities last.

Your Privacy—The Harlequin® Reader Service is committed to protecting your privacy. Our Privacy Policy is available online at www.ReaderService.com or upon request from the Harlequin Reader Service.

We make a portion of our mailing list available to reputable third parties that offer products we believe may interest you. If you prefer that we not exchange your name with third parties, or if you wish to clarify or modify your communication preferences, please visit us at www.ReaderService.com/consumerschoice or write to us at Harlequin Reader Service Preference Service, P.O. Box 9062, Buffalo, NY 14269. Include your complete name and address.

HAR13R

SPECIAL EXCERPT FROM

H HARLEQUIN®

American Romance®

Read on for a sneak peek at
HIS CHRISTMAS SWEETHEART
by New York Times *bestselling author*
Cathy McDavid

The handsome ranch hand Will Desarro is a man of few
words, but Miranda Staley soon discovers that beneath
that quiet exterior beats a heart of gold.

Miranda grinned. Will Dessaro was absolutely adorable
when flustered—and he was flustered a lot around her.

How had she coexisted in the same town with him for all
these years and not noticed him?

Then came the day of the fire and the order to evacuate
within two hours. He'd shown up on her doorstep, strong,
silent, capable, and provided the help she'd needed to rally
and load her five frightened and uncooperative residents
into the van.

She couldn't have done it without him. And he'd been
visiting Mrs. Litey regularly ever since.

Thank the Lord her house had been spared. The same
couldn't be said for several hundred other homes and buildings in Sweetheart, including many on her own street. Her
beautiful and quaint hometown had been brought to its
knees in a matter of hours and still hadn't recovered five
months later.

"I hate to impose…." Miranda glanced over her shoulder,
making sure Will had accompanied her into the kitchen.
"There's a leak in the pipe under the sink. The repairman
can't fit me in his schedule till Monday, and the leak's

worsening by the hour." She paused. "You're good with tools, aren't you?"

"Good enough." He blushed.

Sweet heaven, he was a cutie.

Wavy brown hair that insisted on falling rakishly over one brow. Dark eyes. Cleft in his chin. Breathtakingly tall. He towered above her five-foot-three frame.

If only he'd respond to one of the many dozen hints she'd dropped and ask her on a date.

"Do you mind taking a peek for me?" She gestured toward the open cabinet doors beneath the sink. "I'd really appreciate it."

"Sure." His gaze went to the toolbox on the floor. "You have an old towel or pillow I can use?"

That had to be the longest sentence he'd ever uttered in her presence.

"Be right back." She returned shortly with an old beach towel folded in a large square.

By then, Will had set his cowboy hat on the table and rolled up his sleeves.

Nice arms, she noted. Tanned, lightly dusted with hair and corded with muscles.

She flashed him another brilliant smile and handed him the towel.

His blush deepened.

Excellent. Message sent and received.

Will Miranda lasso her shy cowboy this holiday season?
Find out in
HIS CHRISTMAS SWEETHEART
by New York Times *bestselling author Cathy McDavid*
Available November 5, 2013,
only from Harlequin® American Romance®.

American Romance

To Love, Honor…and Multiply!

Becoming a husband and family man in the middle of a
raging land feud wasn't the destiny Galen Callahan saw for
himself. But once he laid eyes on Rose Carstairs, he knew
the bouncy blonde with the warrior heart was his future.
Now, with Rancho Diablo under siege, the eldest Callahan
sibling will do whatever it takes to protect his new wife
and triplets. With Callahan lives and legacy on the line,
Galen has a new mission: to vanquish a dangerous enemy
and bring his family together in time for Christmas!

A *Callahan Christmas Miracle*
by *USA TODAY* bestselling author
TINA LEONARD

**Available November 5,
from Harlequin® American Romance®.**

HARLEQUIN®

American Romance®

A Small Town Thanksgiving
by MARIE FERRARELLA

Ghostwriter Samantha Monroe has just arrived
in Forever, Texas, to turn a remarkable woman's
two-hundred-year-old journals into a personal memoir.
The Rodriguez clan welcomes her with open arms…
and awakens Sam's fierce yearning to be part of a family.
But it's the eldest son, intensely private rancher
Mike Rodriguez, who awakens her passion.

Delving into the past has made Sam hungry for a
future—with Mike. The next move is up to him—if he
doesn't make it, the best woman to ever happen to him
just might waltz back out of his life forever!

**Available November 5,
from Harlequin® American Romance®.**

HAR75479

Love the Harlequin book you just read?

Your opinion matters.

Review this book on your favorite
book site, review site, blog or your own
social media properties and share
your opinion with other readers!

HREVIEWS